ADVENTURES
OF
DIRTY
DOTTIE

ADVENTURES
OF
DIRTY DOTTIE

FINDING JOY

CAROLYN
SCHIELD

TOM
VORBECK

ACKNOWLEDGEMENTS

Special thanks to our outstanding copy editor, Kay Gambill, for her incredible patience and talent. Her dedication over the years inspired us to continue with our dream. Her tremendous courage and honesty were much appreciated.

Thank you to our assistant editor/test reader/proofreader, Anna Grayson, for her kindness and time. She did a fantastic job filling all of her roles to assist us in bringing our story to reality.

We thank Mark Oliver for combining his talents with Tom to produce a stunning cover.

To our spouses, Jennifer and John, thank you for believing in us and encouraging us through the long writing process. You gave us time and space and often were sounding boards. Your love and unwavering support provided us the freedom to pursue this journey.

To our father, mother, and brother, thank you for always being in our corner and encouraging us to follow our dreams. We feel your smiles of pride.

And finally, thanks to our fans. Your love for and curiosity about Dottie touched us and inspired us to pursue these adventures and unveil her story.

Family, friends, fans, and our writing team, thanks to all of you, we did it! Again!

CONTENTS

CHAPTER 1

⚜

GREAT DAY

Dirty Dottie was an enigma to many and certainly a picture of contradictions. The outside world often saw her strength and confidence, but in private moments, one might see her vulnerability. She could make men blush with her double entendres and yet soothe troubled souls with her angelic singing. She gave the appearance of living a carefree life when it was her mission to do right and defend right. She had a timeless beauty about her. Her life experiences suggested she was a woman in her sixties, but her long, flowing, blond hair and curvaceous, toned body told another story. When some would dare to question her age, Dottie always responded with a knowing smile, "Polite folks don't ask, and a lady never tells." With that, she would wink her eye, blow a kiss, and saunter away, leaving her mystery in her wake.

Dottie finished another day of grueling rehearsals. She looked forward to her evening with her husband but needed a rest and spruce up before he got home and Act One began. Changing from her sweaty theater clothes to her husband's favorite black teddy, Dottie reclined on a chaise lounge and sipped a vintage wine. She hummed the new song for her show; it still needed work, but it was getting there. Seeing the mail stacked on the antique side table, Dottie sighed in resignation. *It's time to go through this mess. Junk. Junk. Junk. What a waste!*

Suddenly, she sat up. In her hand was an envelope with a return address that she recognized. Removing her small dagger from its sheath, she sliced open the envelope in one quick motion. It was an invitation to a party celebrating the twins' first birthday. Inside the card was a handwritten note that read:

Dottie,

As we prepare to celebrate the twins' first birthday, it is with a joyous heart that my thoughts rest on you with gratitude and heartfelt thanks. This celebration would not be possible if it were not for you. Indirectly, you have managed to save all our lives and, in some cases, multiple times. I am not the first to say that you have a larger-than-life personality. However, deep inside you, I see the purest of hearts. That makes you one of us and part of our family. I pray that this invitation finds you well.

Thanks for saving my ass and my Ash.

You will always have my unconditional love.

*I pray that you will come and join **YOUR** family. It will not be a great day without our Dirty Dottie.*

Love,

Cordy

Happy tears streamed down Dottie's face. She had many accomplishments, but none fulfilled her desire to be part of a family. She could never have children and yearned for a family bond and connectedness. Cordy and her family were offering her the desire of her heart. Finally, she had a family she could call her own.

"Damn that Cordy!" Dottie chuckled; few people could get the tough-as-nails Dottie to cry.

As she dried her eyes and wiped away her mascara, she heard the bedroom door open. Seeing that she had been crying, her husband rushed to her side. With alarm, he asked, "What's wrong, honey?"

"Nothing is wrong! It's all wonderful! I just received an invitation to the twins' birthday party. You remember—Ash's one-year-old twin brother and sister. Cordy included a personal note. She told me she loves me and considers me part of their family. So, everything is okay. In fact, it's a great day!

"I've got to get packing! I have a party to get to in Nova Scotia! My tribe is waiting for me!"

For many, receiving an invitation on such short notice would throw them into a panic. Not Dottie. She was a lady of action! She called and expedited her one-way plane ticket, collected her necessary travel documents, hurriedly packed her suitcase, and was on the plane en route to Nova Scotia in a few short hours.

When Dottie landed in Nova Scotia, she grabbed her bag and headed to the hotel for a quick nap. She set the alarm on her watch, forgetting she was now in the Atlantic Time Zone. After a few hours, her alarm buzzed. Still suffering from jetlag, getting up and getting ready took an enormous effort. She stumbled around, searching for the shoes she had kicked off earlier, and noticed the clock on the nightstand.

"Bloody hell! I forgot to adjust the time on my watch! I'm going to be late!"

Dottie jumped into a taxi and gave the driver the address. She explained, "I'm in a hurry! I'm attending a very important event, so if you get me to that address in thirty minutes, I'll give you a hundred-dollar tip."

"No problem!" assured the driver. "I'm your man." With that, he stomped the gas pedal, propelling Dottie back against her seat. Once anchored and settled, she noticed the fine male specimen behind the wheel. She commended him on his excellent control and ability to maneuver the sharp curves at such a high speed. His good looks and his skill were two qualities Dottie found alluring. With a wicked smile, she thought, *I appreciate a man who can maneuver my sharp curves—fast or slow—just as long as we get to the finish line.*

Dottie gazed out the window as they sped down the road. She became lost in memories as she viewed the beautiful coastline. Her new family wasn't aware that she knew Chief Saunhac, chief of the Mi'kmaq tribe and Cordy's great-grandfather. Dottie worked with him when they both were younger. She recalled him as a handsome young man who knew how to fill out a military uniform. More importantly, he understood that evil existed. Ruthless men and women would go to extreme lengths to steal artifacts and artwork believed to hold supernatural qualities. He made it his mission to thwart their efforts by finding as many mystical treasures as possible and stowing them in the natural hiding places in his homeland of Nova Scotia. Dottie frequently assisted him in his quest.

Even at ninety years old, Chief Saunhac had continued his mission. His noble work came to an unexpected end when a Dark

Watcher sniper assassinated him. Dottie's eyes clouded with tears as she remembered the old chief's untimely demise and the hole it left in Cordy's heart.

The taxi driver's triumphant voice interrupted Dottie's memories, "The GPS indicates we are ten minutes out! I should make my tip by two minutes!"

CHAPTER 2

⚜

LET'S PARTY!

The party day finally arrived! Mary, the housekeeper, and her granddaughter baked a cake and prepared a feast. Mary commandeered Little Louie, a tall Mi'kmaq man, to hang the decorations. Balloons and crepe paper hung everywhere. It had been a while since the family had been together, and Aziza and Han anxiously awaited their guests' arrival.

This gathering was much more than a birthday celebration. It also was a celebration of endurance and survival. Aziza and Han had endured much in their married life. They were both blessed with talents that eventually led to their years-long separation.

Aziza was Ash's mother. She was an Egyptian woman now living in Nova Scotia. She was stunning with her thick, ebony hair and dark chocolate brown eyes. She had the gifts of intuitive insight, healing, and seeing the future. Most of the time, she considered her gifts blessings, but they could be a curse. Sometimes her visions were heartbreaking, and she could do nothing to alter them.

Han was Ash's father. In his younger days, Han was a gifted archeologist at the University of Kiel. One of his assignments was a dig site near Aziza's Egyptian home. Aziza's dark-haired beauty caught his eye, but her brilliant intellect and innate kindness captured his heart.

Han was older than Aziza, but she preferred a mature man. They married and had a son named Ash. When Ash was young, his father discovered a cave that contained a legendary, cursed star room. While excavating the cave, it collapsed and swallowed Han into a shaft. Boulders wedged themselves above, preventing any entrance. Rescue teams attempted to dig through the rubble, but their efforts were fruitless. As the site became more treacherous, the authorities finally ended their search. Even though they never recovered Han's body, the government declared him dead.

Ash followed in his father's footsteps, becoming a noted archeologist specializing in Egyptian archeology. The Pure of Hearts, a secret organization, recruited him to locate and retrieve relics and artifacts believed to have supernatural powers. The Children of the Nephilim, a sinister group desiring world dominion, coveted these relics. They believed these unique items would ensure their rise to power. Ash and his compadres retrieved the relics and hid them away to prevent them from falling into the wrong hands. While pursuing them, Ash discovered his father was still living. Han revealed he disappeared to protect Aziza and Ash after agreeing to work for the Pure of Hearts, the organization Ash now served. After twenty-five years, Ash, Aziza, and Han reunited. The twins were born some months later, increasing their family to five.

In his relic quest, Ash met his wife, Cordy. She, too, received the call to locate and retrieve relics and artifacts. They joined forces and formed a band of associates that assisted them in the fight. Ultimately, Ash, Cordy, and their team defeated the Children of the Nephilim, and the world was safe for now. However, like the ancient Greek mythical character, Lernaean Hydra, which grew back two heads for each one severed, the Pure of Heart and the Light Watchers knew that the Children of the Nephilim would soon regenerate their evil agenda and be a force to reckon with once again.

Bill McDermott, Cordy's grandfather, also attended the party. He, too, played a major role in the battle against the Children of the Nephilim, serving as the CEO of the Light Watchers until he retired last year.

Ash's friend Remington, a six-foot, seven-inch Welsh Native American, unwittingly joined the party when he arrived unexpectedly bearing a crate containing what he believed to be the Tablets of Stone. He explained to Ash that a comrade in arms instructed him to deliver the parcel to him and his father. Curious at its contents but not wanting to take the attention away from the twins, Ash and Han suggested they examine it after the party.

Due to work responsibilities, Bob and Julia, honorary aunt and uncle, could not attend the celebration. They sent a giant teddy bear that nearly filled the playroom and arranged a telecom meeting so they could be a part too.

Family and friends, in person and electronically, gathered around the birthday cake and sang to the twins. They watched as Aziza opened the presents. When she got to the last small package, she announced it was from 'Aunt Dirty Dottie.'

Han wondered, "Dirty Dottie. Isn't she a friend of yours, Ash?"

"Yes, Dottie is a friend of mine. She saved my life several times during our quest to defeat the Children of the Nephilim and protect the treasures of the Pure of Heart.

"Dottie has exceptional skill at attention to detail. I guess she remembered the twins' birth date from the picture you sent me when I hid on her boat. Notice her new title, 'Aunt.' It looks like she's adopted our family as her own. That's OK with me. She is one special woman!" Ash beamed fondly.

Cordy cautioned, "Be careful, Aziza. Be very careful when you open that package. Dottie is a bit on the wild side."

Ash laughed, putting his arm around his wife, "A bit?!"

Aziza tore away the paper and hesitantly opened the box. She removed two matching sippy cups that resembled round breasts with nipples. Michael clapped excitedly and reached for one of them.

Han turned beet red. Wanting to respect Dottie's gesture toward his children, he choked out, "Oh, aren't those nice? How sweet of her. I see there is something else in the box. It's a CD labeled *Aunt Dirty Dottie sings "Happy Birthday."*

Distracting Michael, Aziza returned the cups to the box. "Oh good! She included a gift receipt. For the Sex Toy Novelty Shop?!"

Everyone broke out into hysterical laughter.

With twinkling eyes, Ash consoled his parents. "It's probably the only toy shop she visits regularly. We better check the disc before letting the babies hear it."

Bill cackled. "It's only "Happy Birthday." What could she do?"

With trepidation, Ash picked up the disc and inserted it into the CD player. "I warn you. There's a reason she's called Dirty Dottie."

Han urged Ash, "Well, the suspense is killing me. If you're that worried about the twins, we'll cover their ears while we listen to it. Push the button already!"

They listened with their hands over the twins' ears as Dottie's sultry voice filled the room. Her rendition of "Happy Birthday" conjured memories of a beautiful blond serenading a long-ago president.

Grandpa Bill patted his heart and panted, "I stand corrected. I bet she has brought many men to their end with her siren song."

As they finished listening to the disc, Aziza stopped and seemed to stare into space.

Cordy quickly went to her side and asked, "Mama Aziza, are you all right?"

"Yes, I'm fine. You know I get glimpses of the future."

"Yes, I know that."

"I just had a glimpse. I see a surprise visitor coming to our door."

Cordy innocently looked down toward the floor and whispered, "Is Dottie coming?"

Aziza smiled, "I believe she is very close."

A few minutes before she arrived at Chief Saunhac's home, Dottie checked her make-up and adjusted her push-up bra, generously exposing her cleavage. She jumped from the taxi and paid the fare, including the hundred-dollar tip. She complimented the driver on a well-done job and sprinted to the door.

The doorbell chimed, startling them. "I wonder who that could be? Everyone is already here," Mary murmured as she crossed the room to answer the door.

Cordy announced, "What would a party be without a surprise? Wait till you see who our special guest is!"

Mary opened the door. Before her stood a smiling Dottie wearing her signature plunging neckline, skin-tight dress, and stiletto heels. They all gaped as the mysterious beauty sashayed through the door and sauntered into the room as if she owned it.

Aziza recovered before Cordy and Ash could make introductions. This was the lady she had seen in her vision. This had to be Dirty Dottie! Aziza threw her arms around Dottie and pulled her in for a hug. "You're the woman who saved my son's life. We owe you so much! Thank you, thank you!" She pulled back to let Dottie take a breath.

Dottie shook her head, "No thanks needed. It's what I do."

As soon as Aziza released Dottie, Cordy embraced her, kissed her cheek, and whispered, "Welcome home, Auntie."

"Oh my gosh!" exclaimed Ash as he lifted Dottie off her feet and swung her in a circle of happiness. "Cordy and I are so happy to see you!"

"And it is so good to see my Ash man again," as she shamelessly squeezed his backside.

Ash blushed, "Everyone, this is the sensational Dirty Dottie. My sweet lady, to what do we owe the pleasure of your visit?"

With a hitch in her voice, Dottie explained, "This is all Cordy's doing. Cordy, you can't imagine how happy you made me by including me in your family celebration."

Everyone started talking at once, welcoming her, inviting her further into the room to join the party. Their unconditional welcome touched her. It wasn't just Cordy who accepted her as family. They all did; no questions asked, no restrictions. They loved her for who she was. Wiping away the tear that threatened to escape, Dottie gave herself a pep talk—*Dry it up, girl. You have a party to attend and family bonds to forge.*

Ash asked Cordy, "How did you know it would be Dottie at the door?"

"Your mother's gift."

Dottie overheard Ash's question and said, "Oh, I have some hidden talents and special gifts I can share with you girls."

Cordy laughingly explained, "Dottie, Dottie, not those kinds of gifts. Aziza occasionally has visions of the future. She saw your approach."

As the evening progressed, the twins' irritability increased. Recognizing the signs of an impending meltdown, Aziza announced it was the twins' bedtime. Although she preferred to whisk them straight to bed, they required a bath as icing covered them from head to toe. Aziza and Cordy each took a hand of a twin and headed down the hall. Cordy turned back and looked at Dottie, "Would you like to join us?"

With gratitude, Dottie smiled and nodded her head yes. She asked Aziza, "May I tell them a bedtime story after their bath?"

Aziza looked over at Cordy with uncertainty. Cordy mouthed to Aziza, "No worries. I got this."

"How about a lullaby instead, Dottie? You have such a wonderful voice," Cordy suggested.

"Oh, I can't wait. This day keeps getting better and better." Ignoring their stickiness, she collected the twins in her arms, squeezed them tightly, and took charge. "Come on, you two. It's the tub for you." With a twin in each arm, she marched down the hall.

Dottie insisted she could manage the twins on her own. She shooed Aziza and Cordy back to the living room. Exhausted, Aziza and Cordy appreciated the break, but more, Dottie's singing brought such pleasure and comfort. She went from one song to another, entertaining and soothing the twins. As she tucked them in, she crooned the song "In the Arms of an Angel." Each person stilled as her voice lilted to the front of the house, each one swept away in their memories.

Aziza whispered, "She cannot know what that song means to me." Putting her arm around Aziza, Cordy pulled her close and shared the memory. During a terrible storm, Aziza went into premature labor. Fallen debris blocked the roads, preventing the prompt arrival of the three paramedics. Too far progressed to risk driving to the hospital, the twins were born at home. However, there were complications. The twins' vital signs dropped, Gabrielle became nonresponsive, and Aziza had seizures. The paramedics acted quickly, each gathering a precious life in their arms. Immediately, Michael's vital signs improved, Gabrielle started breathing, and Aziza's seizures stopped. The paramedics' healing embrace saved them. Aziza would always be grateful to those angels; without them, she and the twins would not have survived.

When the song was over, Dottie tip-toed out of the nursery. She paused for a moment, emotion overwhelming her. Those twins—they were the most loving audience she had ever had. "This family is mine, something I have wanted my entire life."

Wiping another tear that threatened to slip away, Dottie straightened her dress, adjusted her cleavage, and strutted to the kitchen to join the others.

CHAPTER 3

EXTRAORDINARY FIND

While Aziza and Cordy rested and Dottie bathed the twins, Mary and her granddaughter began the cleanup. The men gathered in the library to examine Remington's mysterious container.

Han put on his glasses and adorned a pair of white gloves. Opening the crate, he found a stone box inside. As he touched the sides of the second lid, the plain top began to glow, and words slowly appeared. Awestruck, Han looked closely and proclaimed, "These are Jesus' two great commandments. 'Thou shalt love the Lord thy God with all thy heart, and with all thy soul, and with all thy mind....Thou shalt love thy neighbor as thyself (Matthew 22:37-39).'"

Ash marveled, "a holy reminder that compassion for our fellow man is one of the keys of life."

As Han slowly raised the second lid, a bright light beamed underneath it, illuminating two stone tablets resting on the bottom of the box. He carefully set the lid aside and delicately lifted the tablets to examine them. "These tablets are exquisite and in re-markable condition. They appear to be lapis lazuli." Running his gloved fingers over the surface, he felt indentations. He asked Ash to hand him his magnifying glass.

While the men waited in quiet anticipation, Han scrutinized every detail, moving the magnifying glass as if he were reading something. In wide-eyed wonder, he looked up and said to his companions, "These could be the Tablets of Stone, the Ten Com-mandments!

"The Ark of the Covenant housed the tablets. Remington, if these are authentic, how did these come into your possession? The Holy Bible teaches that no person can touch the ark. It would be instantaneous death."

Remington recounted his harrowing journey. "The Dark Watch-ers captured me and imprisoned me in an underground bunker. After overcoming a few challenges, Ash and his buddy finally rescued me. We then escaped to Dirty Dottie's showboat. While discussing our shared mission to rescue Pure of Heart treasures, Uriel, the red-haired angel, appeared. He directed me to flee Dottie's boat and seek a valuable relic in my homeland. I had to go over the side and swim to shore before the Dark Watchers stormed the boat.

"It took me a while, but I finally found the cave housing the tablets. Inside, I saw what appeared to be an open ancient chest. Standing next to it, like a sentry, was Uriel, holding the tablets. He handed them to me and told me to bring them to you; you would know what to do with them.

"Han, I never touched the open chest beside Uriel. I packed the tablets as Uriel instructed and brought them directly to you and Ash."

Patting him on the shoulder, Han said, "You've done well, Re-mington."

With a solemn countenance, Han continued, "Gentlemen, we have an extraordinary find before us. I don't think any of us would disagree that these are some sort of a Pure of Heart treasure. We must keep them in hiding to prevent them from falling into evil hands. I know a place we can temporarily store them. I found one of Chief Saunhac's hiding places here in the house. I'll keep them there until a permanent location is determined."

As Han repacked the tablets, he suggested that Ash, Reming-ton, and the rest of the men wait for him in the kitchen. "I'll join you after I secure these precious items. I think tonight's discovery calls for a drink!"

CHAPTER 4

HOW DOTTIE BECAME DIRTY DOTTIE

Mary, her granddaughter, and the men sat around the kitchen table discussing the significance of Remington's find when Dottie's loving voice floated into the room. Everyone stopped talking and let her comforting voice envelope and soothe them.

Regretting having to break the mood, Louie cleared his voice and softly said, "I'm going to have to leave. I'm leading the sunrise ceremony in the morning and must make the final preparations.

"Remington, you're welcome to bunk with me and join us in our celebration if you're not opposed to getting up early."

Remington warmly accepted the invitation.

As everyone exited their chairs, Dottie strolled in with Cordy and Aziza behind. Dottie demanded, "What's a girl gotta do to get a drink around here?"

The men jumped as one, stumbling over themselves, trying to pull out a chair for her. They talked over each other as they offered her a variety of drinks. Cordy chuckled as she watched the men succumb to Dottie's charm and behave like schoolboys vying for the heart of the prom queen.

Cordy hugged Dottie and apologized, "Dottie, Aziza and I are exhausted. As much as we would love to share a nightcap with you and your fawning admirers, we're 'done in.' We'll see you in the morning."

Cordy leaned over Ash's shoulder and planted a smacking kiss on his cheek. With a wicked smile, she cooed, "Don't be long, Ash man. I'll be waiting for you!" Before heading upstairs with Aziza, Cordy wagged a finger at Dottie and playfully scolded, "Behave yourself, young lady!"

"Oh, Cordy, you don't have anything to worry about. Tonight, I'm just one of the boys! They don't have anything that I haven't seen before."

Cordy stopped mid-step as she remembered Grandpa Bill was an eligible bachelor. She cautioned him, "Grandpa Bill, be good! If you can't be good, be careful! Dottie is a sneaky one! You'll never see her coming!"

Dottie chortled, "Don't worry, honey. When I come, everyone knows it!"

Cordy and Aziza rolled their eyes and headed to bed.

Mary, her granddaughter, Little Louie, and Remington said their goodbyes and called it a night.

Ash, Han, and Bill remained at the table with Dottie. Han rooted under the kitchen sink and discovered a fifth of Kentucky whiskey. He held it up, inquiring if it was an acceptable choice. They agreed it was perfect for the occasion. Han removed the seal with grand ceremony and poured half-portions into large glasses.

"Han, you don't mess around when filling a girl up. I like that in a man."

Dottie raised her glass and proposed a toast, "Here's to survival!

"Gentlemen, who would have dreamed that the four of us would end up together in the same room? I believe I have rescued all three of you from some watery misfortune.

"Ash man, do you recall how you staggered from the river half naked? Bare-chested, slick, and wet, your skin glistening in the moonlight, your trousers molding every bulge perfectly. Ahhh, a gift from God for these eyes to behold!"

Blushing, Ash pleaded, "Now, Dottie, let's not go there!"

Intrigued by Dottie's innuendo directed at Ash and his blush, Han and Bill seemed to overlook Dottie's comment about previously rescuing them. They encouraged Dottie to continue her tale involving Ash, "Oh, let's go there!"

Hoping to distract the two overly curious cronies, Ash asked Dottie, "How did you get the name Dirty Dottie?"

"Well, my Ash man, it's an amusing story. Most people think I was born in the United Kingdom because of my British accent. Actually, I'm from a small village in the Middle Eastern town of Sychar.

"During the summer, we swam in a small lake on the village's west side. Our culture prohibited girls and boys from swimming together, so the village elders created a swimming schedule. Girls swam first. Then after a break, the boys could swim.

"On a scorching day, I took advantage of our swimming time. I swam for two hours, dreaming of a life outside the village. When the horn blared, signaling the end of the girls' swimming time, I wasn't ready to leave my cool oasis to return to reality. I hid under the dock until all the girls were gone. I swam back out, intending to float for a few moments longer but lost track of time in my solitary musings. The horn blared again, announcing the boys' time, startling me to awareness.

"I frantically swam to the dock, hoping to make a quick exit before any of the boys arrived. But no such luck! Standing three abreast, blocking my way, were the notorious three. Obelisk, nicknamed Obel, was the ringleader. His followers were Daneg and Alvan.

"I had no option but to get out of the water and walk past them. Confidently, I emerged from the water like a triumphant mermaid, water sliding over my sun-glistened skin. The three miscreants froze in place, their mouths gaping as I hurriedly toweled off. I was twelve years old with a young woman's body. Even then, I had curves in all the right places, and my wet swimdress accentuated every last one of them.

"It didn't alarm or insult me that they were ogling. With a body like mine, that frequently occurred. What infuriated me was that they wouldn't let me pass!

"Never backing down from a challenge, I stupidly asked them if they were going to say something or just gawk at me all day.

"Recovering from his momentary loss of speech, Obel proposed a stereotypic male pubescent solution. They would let me pass if I played the game 'You show me yours, and I'll show you mine.'

"I was surprised. I thought it would be 'Let's play doctor.' Thinking quickly, something I do superbly well, I might say, I decided to use negotiations and trick them to get me out of the annoying predicament.

"Coyly, I said, 'I'll show you mine, but you must show me yours first.'

"The three hopeful boys put their heads together and discussed my terms. Obel and Alvan appeared to agree, but Daneg kept shaking his head in vehement objection. Finally, they coerced him to acquiesce.

"Turning their backs to me, they shimmied and dropped their trunks. They whirled back around and faced me in all their glory. Hands on their hips, they posed like Greek gods, proudly displaying their manhood. I pretended to admire what was before me, while on the inside, I was laughing hysterically as I mentally rated them. Obel's parents aptly named him Obelisk as he grew into his name right before my eyes. Alvan was mediocre, but poor Daneg was nothing more than a peanut. No wonder he didn't want to participate in the game."

Dottie paused a moment. Ever the show woman, she had her audience right where she wanted them, captivated and hanging on to her every word. She reached across the table, took the whiskey, and started topping off their glasses. Ash attempted to decline and push his glass away politely, but Dottie challenged him, "If I'm going to tell you my secrets and hidden talents, you are drinking with me."

Sliding Ash's glass over for Dottie to refill, Han cajoled Ash, "Now, son, we must oblige our honorary guest. Just a splash more so Dottie will continue her story. She's just getting to the good parts."

Somewhat insulted, Dottie grumbled, "Good parts? I'll have you know I only have spectacular parts; ask Ash. His hands very much appreciated the parts under my dress."

Ash's cheeks flamed red with embarrassment. How was he supposed to discuss this with his father and Cordy's grandfather? He cringed at the thought that his father would tell his mother because he would think the story was hilarious. Even though he was an adult, his mother, a proper lady, wouldn't hesitate to chastise him in the morning.

Ash pleaded, "Oh, Dottie, why did you mention that? You know that was a necessary situation beyond my control. Can't we forget it?"

"OOOOH no!" the two men roared. "You aren't getting off that easy. Spill the beans, Ash."

Ash conceded, "Oh, all right. The sooner I tell you, the sooner Dottie can finish her story, and I can go to bed.

"This happened last year during one of the many times I was on the run from the Dark Watchers. In this particular instance, I eluded them long enough to get to Dottie's showboat. I sprang on deck and hustled to the auditorium, where I could hear her practicing for her next show. Costumed in an old southern belle hoopskirt, she turned to see who rudely interrupted her rehearsal, ready to give the intruder a colorful earful. I shouted that the Dark Watchers were on my heels. Hearing a skirmish down the hall as her security attempted to prevent their boarding, Dottie lifted her skirt and ordered me to climb in. I dove under. She dropped her skirt, completely concealing me."

"Oh, and how he fit in so perfectly, just like two jigsaw puzzle pieces locking together." Dottie wickedly winked at Ash and let out a gleeful cackle.

Emboldened by the alcohol, the playful atmosphere Dottie had created, and the eagerness of the two other men, Ash continued, "I must say, Dottie, I had two surprises that day. The first was your black lacy thong panties, and the second was the hard body inside them. And yes, both were spectacular. I had to hold on to something, didn't I?" Ash winked back at Dottie.

"Yes, you did. I have never had one so young grasp and cradle my bum with such authority and command."

As much as she enjoyed the young pup's embarrassment and banter, it was time to bring her tale to an end. "Well, enough about my Ash man and our little adventure under my skirts. Let me finish this up.

"Obel impatiently demanded that I keep my end of the bargain. I had to figure out how to use my wiles to manipulate these three hooligans into switching positions with me so that I had a clear path to escape. I began singing a sultry song. Using my towel like a silk scarf, I danced in a circle, maneuvering them so that now they were at the water end of the dock, and I was in front of them. Now my path was clear. In the best temptress voice a twelve-year-old could conjure, I told them to turn around and prepare for my unveiling. They enthusiastically complied. I backed away silently as they faced the water and kicked their feet in anticipation. That was my undoing!

"I'd only gotten a few steps away when I slipped and plummeted face-first into the sticky black goo surrounding the dock. I stood up but couldn't get my footing and fell backward. Covered with mud from head to toe, I finally regained my balance and bolted away as fast as possible. As I sprinted through the streets, all the people yelled, 'Look at that Dirty Dottie run!' From that day on, just like the mud, the name stuck.

"That's how I became Dirty Dottie. Nothing torrid or nefarious like most people think. Just a clumsy fall into a pool of mud."

Ash rose from his chair and went around and embraced Dottie. "Thank you for insisting I stay to hear the end of your informative tale. Know this, dear lady. You are Dottie to us, just Dottie!

"Now, I bid you all adieu. My wife is waiting for me." Ash kissed

Dottie's cheek and walked the walk of the slightly inebriated out of the kitchen.

"Well, boys, are you up for more tale-telling, or do you need your beauty sleep?" teased Dottie.

"I can manage if this old man can," taunted Bill.

"Who're you calling old? Of course, I'm in," groused Han.

Pleased she had stirred these two old war horses into a dither, she finished her story.

"Obel eventually caught me, but not until I was fifteen. I married him. At that time, it was customary for girls my age to marry. Both virgins, we celebrated the passion of young love, innocently believing we had a lifetime ahead of us. Six months later, the army recruited him. He died two days after going to the battlefield.

"I later married Alvan. His stability and business acumen attracted me. What I didn't realize was that he was a workaholic. Alvan didn't have time to invest in our emotional relationship. He believed that he was doing his duty by generously providing for me. One night he was working late. Thieves broke into his place of business and murdered him. We were married for two years when I became a widow again.

"As you may have guessed, Daneg became my third husband. I had no intention of ever marrying again. I didn't want to suffer another loss, and after Alvan, I needed to re-establish my independence. My mother instilled independence in me, but I allowed him to take it away. I couldn't disappoint her, but more importantly, I couldn't disappoint myself. Daneg understood all that about me. He never pressured me. He was just there, tenderly encouraging me, tenderly building me up. I guess you can say he did the old-fashioned thing and courted me. Before I knew it, his compassionate, unconditional love won me over, and I fell in love with him. He sensed when I was ready and popped the question. Of course, I said yes, but I regretted wasting so much time trying to avoid falling in love with him, especially when, two months later, he died from cardiac arrest. I was a widow for the third time.

"I learned a valuable lesson after being married to all three troublemakers at such a young age. Size does matter, but not in the manner you think. It's the size of a man's heart and how he loves that gives the pleasure of a lifetime.

"Daneg's heart gave me that unexpected pleasure. He loved me unconditionally. It made no difference to him if I was Dirty Dottie or just Dottie. In his tenderness and his respect for me, he made me feel treasured. I certainly treasured him. We only had a few months, but Daneg exhibited the love I craved and realized I deserved. I vowed never again to be someone's duty nor settle for less than the 'heart love' that Daneg had given me.

"It was a long time before I found that kind of love again."

CHAPTER 5

YOUNG DEATH,
BROKEN HEART

Moved by Dottie's somber reflection, Han offered comfort and encouragement. "Dottie, you endured so much at such a young age. That painful start could have negatively defined you, but you were resilient. You survived. You persevered."

"Death has been a frequent companion in my life, Han. My earliest memories center around death.

"My first experience with death was shortly after I was born. My parents succumbed to a local plague, leaving me an orphan. When the villagers discovered us, my parents had been dead a whole day. They extricated me from my mother's stiffened arms, listless and barely breathing.

"What were the village elders to do with me? I had no other family. Every family in the village struggled to support themselves due to rampant poverty. Some feared I'd bring a curse upon them because I came from a plague family. Some even suggested returning me to my parents to die with them.

"A miraculous thing occurred. Perhaps the poorest person in the village volunteered to adopt me. Nearly blind and having to beg for food, she had no resources to raise a child, but she had a compassionate heart that surpassed all others.

"My adoptive mother's name was Ma'at, an Egyptian name meaning truth. She related to my situation, someone undesired and abandoned. You see, a year before, at the age of twelve, marauders raided our village and viciously attacked and raped her. They gouged her eyes so she couldn't identify them and left her to die. Somehow she survived, but with the shame of rape, the villagers ostracized her. She fled to the outskirts and lived in isolation as her wounded eyes healed. Scarred and with limited vision, she was determined to make a self-sufficient life for herself.

"At the age of thirteen, that vision-impaired adolescent girl adopted me. Having nothing more than the clothes on her back, she begged for old scarves, discarded baby clothes, and nappies. When a few kind souls provided her with those few meager items, she cradled me in her arms and lovingly carried me to the lean-to where she lived. At night, she sneaked into a goat herd to get milk to feed me.

"Three months later, the villagers were astonished to find me alive and thriving. Some believed God was blessing us. Out of guilt, shame, or spiritual influence, who knows, a few began sporadically donating food scraps and clothes their children had outgrown. Another woman, Kem, let us sleep under her covered back porch when it rained as long as we vacated by early morning.

She didn't want anyone to know that she was helping us. We were still dealing with narrow-minded thinking, but at least we had a dry place to sleep.

"There was no mother in the village better than my mother. Although young and vision-impaired, she did everything you would expect any experienced mother to do. When the food donations ran low, she begged and scavenged to ensure I had enough to eat, often sacrificing her portion for me. She struggled to haul water from the lake to heat it to bathe me. When our lean-to could not withstand bad weather, she always found us shelter. It might have been a nearby cave when Kem's back porch wasn't available, but it was dry, and we were out of the elements. She constantly told me she loved me. She continually demonstrated her love by hugging and snuggling with me. She told me stories, some with life lessons, others just silly. She sang me lullabies and nursery rhymes. For my entire time with her, I felt treasured. I felt secure. I felt loved.

"As I grew, we sang songs together. I had quite a set of pipes, even at the age of four. Once my mother sang a song, I had it memorized. I could sing it back in perfect pitch with emotion beyond my years and understanding. Hating to profit from my exceptional talent but believing this could be a means to support me better, my mother constructed a plan. She convinced one of the farmers to take us to the next town. It was much larger than our humble village, and the people were more affluent. She set us up on a busy street corner. I would sing, and she would work the crowd for donations. I was a cutie. Who wouldn't want to throw some money in a box for an adorable four-year-old with an angelic voice?

"We worked that corner every single week. After two years, my mother finally saved enough money to purchase a small, dilapidated house in our village. It needed work, but it was ours.

"We continued our weekly trips. As I matured, I sensed how I could increase the impact of a song using a hand gesture or a slight body sway. Seeing that the audience enjoyed the addition of the subtle theatrics, I added some dance moves as well. Our coffers increased to where we could purchase a few trinkets for our home and ourselves. I realized that my singing, dancing, and acting skills could be a steady source of income.

"One day, as we worked our corner, a cargo wagon careened down the road out of control. Concentrating on preventing the wagon from toppling over, the driver failed to notice a branch obstructing his path. He ran over it, causing the wagon to buck. He was unaware that a tiny black and white puppy bounced out onto the road. I snatched it up and hollered for him to stop, but he never heard me.

"I lowered the squirming puppy to the ground, but it began whimpering as it limped on its back leg. I scooped it up, wrapped it in my sweater, and raced back to my mother in a terrified panic. She knew exactly what to do. She gently palpitated the puppy's hip and found a slight protuberance. Applying pressure to it, the puppy's hip slipped back into place. A great cry came from the puppy and an agonizing shriek from me. Immediately, the puppy began to frolic and thank us with puppy kisses.

"It wasn't long before the little thing bonded with us and became part of our family. Because she was such a little thing, we named her Little Thing. Everywhere we went, Little Thing went. I taught her a handful of tricks, and we incorporated her into our street performance.

"I was ten when I experienced death again. We were preparing for our show when an expensively dressed man approached my mother. In a polite but arrogant voice, he inquired if he could purchase me. Pushing me behind her, my mother angrily told him I was her daughter and not for sale. She ordered him to move on. Outraged that a handicapped little snippet would speak to him in such a manner and interfere with his desires, he attempted to knock her out of the way and take what he wanted. Little Thing leaped toward him, snarling. Trying to fend off her attack, the man bludgeoned Little Thing with his cane, instantly killing her.

"Enraged and heartbroken, I surged toward the man, pulling out the small knife I had in my pocket. Even then, I carried a knife for utility and protection. Backing away from me, he stumbled over his feet and fell backward, plummeting to the ground.

"I had my arm poised to plunge my knife into his black heart, but my mother struck my arm, upsetting my balance. I fell on top of him, my knife missing his heart but leaving a permanent mark. My little blade mightily sliced the left side of his face, just below his eye, certain to leave an ugly, jagged scar. As my mother screamed for help, the beaten man staggered to his feet, blood dripping down his face. He bolted away, covering the oozing wound with his expensive linen handkerchief before anyone could come to our aid.

"My mother tightly wrapped me in her arms and held onto me with all her strength to prevent me from pursuing the black-hearted murderer. When I finally calmed and no longer struggled against her, she released me so I could pick up Little Thing. Holding our lifeless Little Thing close to my heart, I sat beside my mother. This time, my mother wrapped her arms around me in comfort. We both sat sobbing as we mourned the loss of our Little Thing.

"I may not have killed that man that day, but he will always have the scar to remind him that no one messes with someone I love!

"At eleven, death broke my heart. I had a friend named Nefertiti, but everyone called her Nef. She was the only girl in the village not prejudiced by people's derogatory remarks regarding my mother and me. Over time, we became close friends. We would meet secretly in the late afternoon and talk about our day. Nef always had the most exciting tales as she recounted village gossip.

"One day, Nef didn't show up at our usual spot. Two days became three, and she still didn't come. I worried her parents had discovered our friendship and prohibited her from seeing me because of our status differences. I worried she was sick or hurt. I became so consumed with frantic worry that I couldn't eat or sleep. I decided to take a risk and see if I could find an explanation for her absence. I ventured to her part of the village, keeping out of sight as much as possible because villagers considered me an outcast.

"As I cautiously approached the house I thought to be Nef's, I noticed a sobbing woman striding toward me. I debated what to do. Should I hide, or should I keep on walking? Before making up my mind, the woman hurried toward me, grabbed both my arms, and demanded to know if I was Dottie, the blind woman's child.

"I hesitantly nodded my head yes. She threw her arms around me and explained that she was Nef's mother. She informed me that Nef had developed severe stomach pain three days earlier, confining her to bed. Doctors examined her and discovered a mass in her abdomen. Her prognosis was bleak.

"Nef's mother was coming to find me because Nef told her I was her best friend and was asking to see me. Taking my hand and slowly pulling me toward the house, her mother pleaded with me to return with her. Seeing her pain and wanting to see my only friend, I agreed.

"I timidly tip-toed into Nef's dim room, uncertain what to expect. From piles of puffy pillows, Nef beamed a grateful smile of welcome. I forced a return smile because I had to be brave for her. A single teardrop slid down her pale cheek as she extended a frail hand to take mine and invited me to sit beside her.

"In a labored voice, she said, 'I thought we would have a lifetime of friendship together, but my dearest friend, it isn't to be. Promise me that you will not grieve too long. Remember our special times at our special spot. Maybe you could take a moment each day and visit me there. As the wind touches your face, the bird sings its song, and your heart warms in sweet memories, know I am there listening to you. When I see God, I will thank Him for blessing me with my very special friend, Dottie.'

"And, then, her hand slid out of mine as her breathing slowed to nothing, and her peaceful eyes fluttered closed. In a moment, she was gone. My best friend was gone.

"Brokenhearted and angry, I bounded home with tear-blinded eyes, seeking my mother's loving arms. I wailed at the unfairness of it all. First, I lost my beloved Little Thing, and then I lost my one and only friend, Nef.

"My mother kissed my forehead and tenderly embraced me. She rubbed my back while I sobbed. Once I quieted, she said, 'Little in life is fair, my darling child. What matters is how you deal with what befalls you. You can remain in the dark and surrender to bitterness, or you can remember the light, embrace it, and continue forward. Death is a part of life. Sometimes, it breaks our hearts, but we honor those we've lost by remembering our relationship with them, not drowning in our grief. Remember them, love them, cherish them, and yes, miss them, but always move forward, Dottie. Don't stay in the dark.'

"A year later, I experienced death again. My mother passed from pneumonia."

CHAPTER 6

PAPA DORON

Touched by what Dottie had finished sharing, Bill commented, "Your mother may have been the poorest person in the village, but I didn't hear of anyone with more wisdom or compassion. I can see her influence on how you live your life. Both of you are like the phoenix that rose from the ashes."

"I am so grateful for the foundation she provided me. She taught me to appreciate what I have and not to take anything for granted. She also taught me to be independent and resourceful. Most importantly, she taught me to stay true to myself. She taught me the skills and values I needed to survive, but there was another who gave me what I needed to thrive.

"I never thought when I married Daneg that I would receive double the love. Once I met his father, I understood who had taught him and modeled unconditional love. When we married, his father, whom I affectionately called Papa Doron, loved me like a daughter.

"Papa Doron was a brilliant man, but more than that, he was wise. The villagers often requested that he become a village elder. He always declined because he felt his calling was teaching. He taught small classes in the village until Daneg was old enough to be on his own. Then, he accepted a teaching position in Egypt.

"Even though Papa Doron worked in a big city in Egypt, his heart was in our village. He was forward-thinking in most ways. But, when it came to me, one he loved as a daughter, he was very traditional. After Daneg passed, Papa Doron permanently moved back to Sychar. He felt it was his responsibility to see to my care. I strongly objected to him thinking I couldn't care for myself, and I never wanted him to give up the career he loved. I can still hear his Middle Eastern accent as he insisted, 'Dottie, this is what a father does for his daughter.'

"So, we became roomies. Most of the time, we lived our day-to-day lives in harmony. I acquiesced to his need to take care of me as long as it didn't threaten my independence. When that happened, I respectfully dug in my high heels. He quickly saw that I didn't require his physical care. What he came to realize during our evening chats was that I was no airhead. I had opinions based on facts, not societal expectations. I analyzed individual events and made reasonable interpretations or suggested reasonable solutions. Again, in his Middle Eastern accent, he heralded, 'My god! You are a fountain of untapped intellect! This is where I help you. I give you education, more knowledge. You will go far!'

"Papa Doron kept his vow. He tutored me at night using college-level material. His passion and his teaching skills expanded my world. I consumed information like a starving person consumed food. A particular strength for me was the acquisition of foreign languages. When I completed my studies, I was fluent in French, German, Russian, Italian, and English.

"It wasn't enough that I completed a course of study; Papa Doron wanted me to have the appropriate culminating certificate. He wanted me to have opportunities that exceeded our small village. An education with proper certification would open doors for me.

"Since Papa Doron tutored me privately, he didn't have access to the final test. Using his resources, he contacted a former colleague from when he taught in Egypt. This professor agreed to bend the rules and add my name to his list of qualifying students so I could take the test along with them.

"I took the test, scoring higher than anyone ever had before. I had my official certificate! I don't know who was prouder, Papa Doron or me.

"As long as I remained in our village, I couldn't do anything with my certificate. Papa Doron encouraged me to pursue avenues in big cities, where gender wasn't an issue, but I wouldn't leave him.

"He didn't want my education or intellect to go to waste, so he referred me to businessmen in nearby towns that were more progressive.

"An import/export business finally hired me because I was multi-lingual. They thought I could be an asset to their foreign-speaking clientele. I learned all aspects of the business, from office work to sales. My specialty was customer relations. With my looks and gift of gab, I could charm sales and purchases out of the most stubborn negotiators and the stingiest of pockets. I also learned quite a bit about importing and exporting, which was useful in later years.

"I was proud to be using the education Papa Doron provided for me and to be learning more. Going to work each day was a joy. Coming home, not so much. I met opposition, prejudice, and jealousy while walking through our village. Most believed that a woman was not to work outside the home. Many women were jealous of my looks and accused me of using my beauty to garner favors, sneering that I was living up to my name, 'Dirty Dottie.' They would shout that no matter how much money I earned or how well I dressed, I was still the girl from the outskirts.

"Oh, how I wanted to retaliate, then knock the dirt off my shoes, and flee the village. But, I would not dishonor my mother or Papa Doron by exhibiting shameful behavior and running away. No one would ever say I was a quitter. I would not allow them to sully what I had accomplished. I lived by my mother's advice and didn't stay in the dark. I held my head high, went to work each day, and came home to the comforting arms of Papa Doron.

"I continued working in the import/export business until Papa Doron started exhibiting symptoms of dementia. He quickly declined and could no longer stay by himself. I remained by his side to meet his every need. I owed him so much, but most of all, I loved him. How could I have done anything less?

"Papa Doron lived a year. Having no relatives other than myself, he bequeathed his entire estate to me. As we lived frugally, I never expected his estate to be as bountiful as it was. In his will, he directed me to use the money as I saw fit.

"Of course, I invested some of it. I was building a nest egg, so I had the means to leave the village when the time was right. I used the remainder of Papa Doron's estate to fund the construction of a high school for both boys and girls.

"I wanted to teach at the school, but the village elders wouldn't allow it. Even though I had the credentials, there was still gender bias, my low-status background, and my presumed reputation that prohibited my consideration for an academic position.

"I would not give up. I wanted to be a part of the school Papa Doron sponsored. I petitioned the village elders to permit me to teach singing, dancing, and theater as part of an extracurricular program. They supported the idea of extracurriculars but were hesitant to let me lead the performance arts section. At the council meeting, it was a tied vote, with one vote remaining. One of Papa Doron's friends was the deciding factor. He winked at me and cast his vote, allowing me to teach.

"As a child, I always enjoyed our street performances and understood that it was a means to support ourselves. But, leading the performance arts program, I saw that there could be power in entertainment. I put on a costume, and I became someone else, a new persona. I put on a costume, and I could make my audience believe anything I wanted them to believe. Add my singing voice and dancing skills, and they were putty in my hands. Another door was opening.

"A while later, I received a letter from the import/export business. They informed me that there was a school in Britain offering a teaching assistant position. The position required someone fluent in multiple languages, including English. They provided me with the contact information if I was interested.

"Interested, was an understatement. I could fulfill Papa Doron's and my dreams of doing more than living a village life. I could utilize my foreign language skills again. I could finally knock the dust off my shoes, leave the village, and go far, as Papa Doron predicted.

"It was harder to leave than I imagined. Growing up, I experienced so much prejudice and hateful vindictiveness. But it was also where I received unconditional love and encouragement to be more than what the village believed I could be. It was the place of my mother and Papa Doron. With tears running down my cheeks, I promised my mother and Papa Doron, 'I will survive. I will thrive.'

"A suitcase in each hand, I walked out of the village with the world to become my stage."

CHAPTER 7

WAR OFFICE

Bill gazed at Dottie, tapping his forehead as if in contemplation. "Dottie, when you arrived today, you and your voice seemed very familiar. With all the excitement of your arrival and the twins' birthday, I didn't get a chance to ask about that."

"I wondered when one of you boys would put the pieces together. I told you it was interesting that we ended up in the same spot today. Pour another round, and I'll continue my story and answer all your questions.

"I wasn't in England very long before the war began. The government provided the funding for my salary. To support the military and cover war costs, the government discontinued any funds they deemed non-essential. My position fell in that category, so the school terminated me.

"I didn't panic about my loss of income. I had several marketable skills, so I had confidence that something would come my way. And it did. Walking home on my last day of school, I noticed a handbill advertising secretarial positions in the local recruiting office. I went straight there. With my previous office experience, they hired me on the spot.

"It was a small office where I performed the typical office tasks. The small-town captain I worked for thought he was quite the stud. He had little respect for women beyond what they could do for him in the bedroom. Enamored with my curves, he constantly made lascivious remarks. As he was leaving the loo one day, I discreetly told him his fly was open. Leering, he said, 'I bet you like my big bazooka, don't you, honey.'

"I couldn't let him get away with that wisecrack. If I did, I'd never have respect in the office. With fire in my eyes and a saccharine smile, I retorted, 'No sir, I only saw a bent BB gun with two dud grenades. I won't tell anyone. My condolences to your wife.' He sputtered and stormed out of the office."

Han and Bill nearly toppled out of their chairs from laughing so hard. Gasping for breath, Han said, "Way to go, Dottie!"

"Shortly after that, I received a transfer order to Major Tony Hebret's office. Now, there was a military man who respected the person for their skills, not their gender. I started as a clerk, but after reading my resume, Major Hebret promoted me to his assistant. Because I processed the highly classified documents that floated past my desk daily, I knew the whereabouts of many of our agents and their targets. He trusted me to take coded notes during his secret meetings. He respected my skills at a time when men thought women had nothing upstairs but boobs and bubbles.

"I made some great friends while working in that office. Mary and Kora were Attagirls. They served as pilots in the Air Transport Auxiliary, ferrying newly produced planes to military airfields.

Their service allowed trained pilots to fight in battle. They didn't always get the recognition they deserved, but they were a great bunch of gals, brave as any man." Dottie raised her glass in salute.

"A frequent visitor to our office was a Canadian officer named Simon Cross. Known for his brilliant military strategy, Major Hebret was grateful to have Simon's insight. The office pool was also appreciative just for his presence. He was Adonis in the flesh but humble. He was charismatic and charming. His smile filled the room with sunshine. All of the young things were on the verge of swooning."

Han and Bill stilled, stunned in disbelief. They both served under Simon Cross in a previous lifetime.

"Finally, your old neurons are beginning to fire and make connections. Let's return to this trip down memory lane and see where we end up.

"During one of their strategic planning sessions, Major Hebret requested my presence. He needed me to translate a message they had intercepted that could impact the direction of their plan. He introduced me to Simon to include me in the discussions. There was an instant attraction between us. We ignored the sexual spark and remained professional and focused during the meeting.

"We dated for a week when Simon proposed. With Herculean resolve, we resisted ripping our clothes off each other. Regardless of our reputations and what people believed was true about Dirty Dottie, neither of us gave away the milk for free. As much passion as there was between us, there was even greater 'heart love.' I hadn't found that love since Daneg. I'd wondered if I would ever have that deep love and sizzle again. I found it with Simon. He knew how to touch my heart and other parts as well." Dottie wiggled her eyebrows.

"Two weeks later, we were married. It was wartime, and waiting for a socially acceptable time to marry was out of the question. Tomorrow might not come. Being a widow three times, I understood the reality of that truth firsthand.

"Major Hebret included me more and more in their strategic meetings. With my knowledge of the contents of top-secret documents, my ability to assimilate and interpret information, and my aptitude for foreign languages, they viewed me as a valuable asset to the team. And I got to go home each night and explore Simon's most gorgeous assets.

"I gradually moved out of the office pool and into Major Hebret's war room. I no longer shuffled papers and filed. I was an integral part of assisting the formation of a clandestine mission. Not only did I assist in the planning, but Major Hebret recruited me to have an active role in the field. He assigned me to T-Force and the Monuments Men."

Simultaneously, Han and Bill slammed their glasses on the table. Bill exploded, "We both were part of those missions!"

"Yes, I know," beamed Dottie.

CHAPTER 8

HAN'S STORY

D elighted she had rattled Han's and Bill's memories again, Dottie went forward with her account. "What a day it was when Field Marshall Montgomery signed the papers for surrender from the Germans. Simon and I stood in the corner of the tent, watching as the anxious German delegation with Admiral Von Friedeberg sat at the table and studied the documents. Hitler was dead. They didn't have the leadership or the resources to continue. They didn't like what they were reading but decided they didn't have any alternative but to agree to the terms of the surrender.

"Although everyone felt victory and relief, a celebration was premature. The fighting was over, but the world still wasn't safe. Russia was now a threat as no one was certain how much German weapons development and technology they had obtained.

"Major Hebret came to me in quite a huff, 'Dottie, bring all the intel we have on Kiel and the professors at the university. Command wants us to apprehend them to prevent them from sharing their research with Russia.'"

Han picked up the story. "Before the war, I was a young archeology professor at the University of Kiel. I hated Hitler and knew Stalin's Russia would be terrible to live under. I never intended to become a soldier, but under duress, the Stasi commanders drafted me to be a soldier in East Germany.

"Shortly after Germany's surrender, Simon recruited me as a spy. I was ecstatic to be part of T-Force. I hated being a German soldier. Even more, I hated supporting a cause I found abhorrent. So, when T-Force offered me the opportunity to spy for them, I heartily accepted. This gave me a chance to set the tables straight. I was serving the side of 'right.' I later discovered that the information I found would aid Operation Epsilon. World War II had ended, but another was in gestation. The Cold War was beginning.

"American and British intelligence received information suggesting that some of the professors and on-staff engineers and scientists at the University of Kiel had worked in Hitler's nuclear program. Their knowledge and expertise would be game changers for the countries desiring world dominance, good or bad. To maintain world peace, it was imperative that their information not fall into the wrong hands. My mission was to infiltrate the collegiate staff under the auspices of returning to my former teaching position and identify all the names of the professors and engineers working on rocket and short-range ballistic missile design.

"As part of the teaching staff, I had free reign to wander the campus. I visited many of the engineers and scientists and chatted with them, seeking information. In my wanderings, I stumbled upon the Russian war room. Peering through a partially closed door, I saw pictures of German scientists and engineers attached to a wall. I overheard the Russian plan to scoop up these specialists and relocate them to Russia, where they already utilized German engineers to build Russian rockets. Unfortunately, I could only hear their intent, not the how or when.

"I sent coded messages to British headquarters, informing them of Russia's plan.

"Then all hell broke loose. The Russians came in the night and started a dragnet of gathering all the engineers and scientists and forcing them onto trains to transport them to Russia. I sent my SOS in code to headquarters and executed my escape plan.

"In all the confusion and my military training, I slipped away easily. The Russians focused on apprehending rocket specialists, scientists, and engineers, not archeologists.

"The plan was I would swim to a yacht for extraction. Simon provided me with the coordinates in an encoded return message. I got to the place where I was to enter the water, and I had a moment's pause. It was dark, and the waters were frigid. What were the chances of my survival? Remembering Stalin used the same oppressive regime playbook as Hitler, I realized freedom at any cost was more important. The Allies needed to know how far the Russian nuclear program had advanced with the help of the captured German scientists. I knew it was a long shot, but I plunged into the water and swam to the designated rescue point.

"Angels must have been aiding me. I treaded water in the frigid temperature for hours. As hypothermia started to take me under, I heard the engines of a yacht."

Dottie interrupted, "Gentlemen, I need to whet my whistle, but let's switch to water. Cordy and Aziza will kill me if I let you two boys fall into your cups."

As they sipped their beverages, Dottie resumed Han's tale from her perspective. "Han, you have no idea the angel assistance we had.

"I was at the helm, carefully monitoring my position, when a strange, bright red-haired, handsome man suddenly stood beside me. Mind you, he wasn't a passenger on my boat. He just appeared. He introduced himself as Uriel.

"Nonplussed by his unexplained appearance, I utilized my wiles to gain information. I flirted with him but to no avail. He was all business.

"He said, 'Dottie, I hear you have a reputation among the men.'

"I turned the wheel and laughed, 'Flattery won't get you in my pants, handsome.'

"He belly-laughed, 'I was speaking of your reputation as a captain, not your reputation with men.'

"Insulted, I pouted, 'Well, bloody hell! I thought you were admiring my exquisite curves and physique when all your flattery is for my sailing skills. I hope I'm not losing my looks.'

"With amusement in his eyes, he assured me, 'No, you're quite a looker.'

"I winked back at him and asked, 'What are you doing here?'

"Uriel explained he was part of the rescue team. He would be our eyes in the night since we couldn't use our lights. As he looked intently into the darkness, it was as if he could see Han. He continued to correct my course, leading us closer and closer. Time was of the essence. Knowing how long our buddy here had been in the water, we feared he would lose consciousness before we rescued him.

"Thick fog made visibility impossible. Rocks were everywhere, masked in the mist, making maneuvering more difficult and dangerous. But with Uriel's night vision, we avoided mishap and sped through it.

"While concentrating on my mission, Uriel casually asked me if I was afraid to die. What a question at a time like this! Was he trying to kill us by distracting me?

"I snarled back at him, 'I'm not afraid of anything, least of all death! I'll show you!' Indignantly, I went full throttle. I would have knocked him off his feet if he hadn't been holding on to the rail. The sudden change in speed brought Simon up on deck, wondering what was happening. He had been below studying new intelligence.

"Pointing my thumb over my shoulder, I informed Simon we had a stowaway, and he was distracting me with nonsense questions.

"Uriel extended his hand and introduced himself to Simon. He explained that he was there to assist the mission. He sensed we were close to Han and ordered me to shut down my engine.

"Simon and Uriel rushed to the side, scouring the distance, searching for Han. Hearing an almost imperceptible cry for help, we located him. That last cry depleted Han's strength, and he started to go under. Simon jumped over the side and swam to him. He grabbed Han around the chest and tugged him back to the yacht. Uriel and I reached down and pulled the unconscious Han onto the deck.

"As Simon climbed back up, he yelled at me to start the engine. He heard boats approaching and saw lights bobbing on the water.

"I raced to the wheel and realized Uriel was no longer anywhere on deck. Just like his sudden appearance, he just as suddenly disappeared. I didn't have time to think about it. I had to get us the hell out of there. With our return, I was grateful for the fog. It concealed us as I went full throttle to rocket us out of enemy territory.

"As we anchored, I saw a flash in the sky. I looked up, and suspended in the air was Uriel, with wings outstretched, holding a flaming sword that lit the sky. He saluted me, and then, poof, he evaporated into the fog. Had I been talking to an angel? I remember thinking it was my imagination or the stress of the mission. All I needed was a stiff drink to settle down and clear my head."

"And, I opened my eyes to the most beautiful angel in all creation. Thank you so much for rescuing me. If it weren't for you, I wouldn't have met my Aziza or had my children." Han bowed his head in gratitude and reverence to Dottie.

Han continued, "Once I was warm, dry, and clear thinking, Simon debriefed me on my mission. He informed me that the information I sent helped put Operation Epsilon in motion. An allied team apprehended ten German scientists believed to have participated in Hitler's nuclear program. Detained in a house in England, allied agents secretly monitored their conversations to determine how close Hitler and his government had come to constructing an atomic bomb.

"Then Simon offered me a new opportunity that would take me out of Germany, where I could utilize my expertise in archeology. He described the war between the Children of the Nephilim and the Pure of Heart, how the Nephilim wanted to steal ancient relics and artwork believed to have supernatural power to use them to assist their desire to establish a one-world order and how the Pure of Heart fought to keep them out of their hands.

"This sounded like Hitler and Stalin all over again. Of course, I said yes. I would do anything required to prevent evil tyranny. Simon sent me to Abu Simbel in Egypt to search for the ancient treasure, the Keys of Life. He said these were critical to the success of the Pure of Heart.

"I knew Abu Simbel was a sacred site. It was a temple constructed so that the sun illuminated a specific chamber for just two days. My mission was to identify that chamber and retrieve its relics.

"You both know this is where I met Aziza, and we started our family. The Nephilim discovered my assignment and put out a hit on us. As I hadn't found the Keys of Life yet, the only thing I could do to protect my family and keep the relics out of the hands of the Nephilim was to destroy what I had excavated and fake my death. Ash was so young when I had to leave.

"Aziza, with her unique gifts, always had a sense that I was alive but no clear picture of where I was. She kept that to herself to keep us all safe, but Ash missed out on having a father in his life. My service to the Pure of Heart was vital, but I regret the time I missed with my son."

Bill nodded, "You made a great sacrifice to protect one of the treasures of the Pure of Heart. Humankind, if they were aware of this secret war, owes you a debt of gratitude. Thank goodness you survived. Cordy and Ash would have never met. It amazes me every time I think of it."

Han pridefully said, "And through Ash, we completed Simon's mission. He found the Keys of Life, and they're now safe, out of the reach of the Nephilim!"

CHAPTER 9

BILL'S STORY

Bill looked at Dottie, "Are you up to any more regaling about adventures with Simon Cross?"

"Of course I am. He is one of my favorite subjects, but after you refill my glass with ice and water. Add a lemon slice to it, please."

Han refreshed their drinks, and Bill began his tale.

"Coming from generations of military men, my father expected me to continue the tradition. To that end, he enrolled me in a private military school rather than a traditional high school, giving me a leg up in basic training. I wasn't quite old enough to enlist when I graduated, so I lied about my age. I was such a babe then. I didn't want to miss the war.

"By the time I completed my basics and specialized training, the Germans had surrendered. I was disappointed because I had been preparing for battle. My disappointment was short-lived when I received orders to deploy to England. Like you, Dottie, I was fluent in several foreign languages, and the higher-ups thought I could be an asset to T-Force.

"When I arrived in England, the Allies were scrambling to grab important personnel and strategic locations. American and British commands had decided Kiel was too valuable to fall into Russia's hands. My first assignment was to assist in coordinating a map of targets.

"My second assignment was under Simon. Both of us being native Canadians, we hit it off immediately. He genially called me Lumberjack in reference to our Canadian roots. Our task was to assist the Monuments Men, a group commissioned to locate and retrieve artworks and treasures stolen or looted by the Germans.

"One of our treks took us to Bad Aussee in Austria. It was known that the Nazis ransacked and confiscated much of the artwork from the country estates in this area. Our intel suggested that some of the paintings were still there, that an SS captain had hidden them rather than dispatched them to Hitler's secret bunkers. Locating the property in question, we heard screams as we pulled up to what was supposed to be an abandoned farmhouse.

"I didn't wait for Simon to come to a complete stop or for him to join me. I bolted out of our vehicle and barreled into the house. The terrified screams were coming from a back bedroom. Entering the room, I witnessed the brutal rape of a young German girl. The rapist's cohorts were watching and drinking, waiting their turn. I withdrew my pistol and, in Russian, ordered them to stop.

"The room became instantly silent. The rapist angrily peered over his shoulder to see who dared to interrupt him. His cohorts stopped mid-drink, stunned by my intrusion. Even the young girl stopped screaming. The silence in the room became deafening as we were all momentarily suspended in time, staring at each other.

Then, I felt the cold steel of a gun pushing into the back of my head. The ringleader was behind the door when I rushed in, not thinking. They all started laughing, and then, as one, stopped.

"I heard the cocking of a gun. Closing my eyes, I prepared to die. Then I heard Simon say, 'No one move, or you'll be wiping this gentleman's brains off your clothes. Lumberjack, walk slowly away and assist the young lady so we can escort her away.' Moving toward the girl, I saw Simon, cool as a cucumber, holding a gun against my executioner's head.

"Once I had the girl covered and away from the men, Simon ordered them all against the back wall. With teeth bared, he glared at the ringleader and said, 'All right, comrades, the fun is over. As long as you behave yourselves, you will live. I know whom you work for, so go back and tell the Chairman of the Children of the Nephilim, Simon Cross says, hello, and I'm coming for him. It's time for us to leave, but first, I believe you have the painting I desire. Where is it?'

"The ringleader responded in practiced English, 'You talk big for one man and one scrawny pipsqueak. We have you outnumbered, English.' With the agility of a ninja, he tucked and rolled across the room, grabbed his gun, and fired at me. I felt the breeze of the bullet brush my cheek. Instinctively, I enfolded the petrified girl and pulled her to the floor. The ringleader stood and aimed at me again as the others scrambled to retrieve their guns. Simon shouted a battle cry and blasted his Thompson submachine gun, killing all but the rapist. I took him out as he cowardly slinked away.

"When the air cleared, the girl ran screaming from the house.

"I'll tell you what, Dottie. Rambo had nothing on our man Simon that day!"

Dottie grinned proudly, "That's my man! Hard and strong just when you need him!"

Shaking his head in amusement, Bill continued the story. "Simon didn't want to leave the house without the painting, but not knowing if we were in friend or foe territory, he didn't want to remain in the area in case the girl alerted anyone. He started to quickly rifle through a closet when I stopped him. I directed him, 'Simon, look under the bed. I noticed it when I was on the floor with the girl.'

"He bent down and withdrew a cloth-wrapped rectangle. Placing it on the table, Simon cautiously removed the cloth, uncovering the painting, *The Astronomer,* mounted in a wood frame. I couldn't believe it. We had just located one of the most treasured artworks by Vermeer. Reverently, Simon said, 'Well, I'll be damned. We found it. This is one painting the Chairman is not getting.' He painstakingly rewrapped the painting, positioned our precious cargo under his arm, and nodded toward the door, signaling it was time to leave.

"As we rushed to our vehicle, I asked about the Chairman; who was he? Simon told me it was a long story and that he'd explain everything once we debriefed back at base.

"As we hauled ass through the countryside, I thanked Simon for saving my life.

"He responded in Simon fashion, advising me to always evaluate a situation before barreling in. I knew that and usually practiced it, but the screams of that young girl evaporated my military training, and my emotions took over. They would have killed me and probably the girl if not for the cool-headed Simon.

"We briefed headquarters of our altercation with the Russian miscreants. We also turned over the Vermeer painting for security.

The powers to be were ecstatic that we had located it, another priceless treasure out of the hands of the Germans.

"After the briefing, Simon suggested we get coffee, and he'd tell me about the Chairman. I was anxious to hear about this unknown enemy.

"Simon explained that according to the Book of Enoch, a group of angels decided to violate the heavenly law where angels were not to interact with women. Some found Eve's daughters beautiful, so they broke the law and took them as wives. The result was the Children of the Nephilim, a hybrid race. Soon, a war ensued as the Children of the Nephilim increased in power and sought the elimination of Adam's children, those who survived the Great Flood extinction event.

"Narcissism, greed, arrogance, and amorality fueled them. Eventually, their hedonistic lifestyle led to the formation of the secret organization, the Children of the Nephilim. They desired to establish a one-world order, as they lusted for total world power and the destruction of the decency of humankind.

"They deceived, stole, raped, pillaged, killed, and over time perverted science and technology to advance their agenda. They infiltrated governments to manipulate policies and actions in their favor. They believed ancient artworks, relics, and treasures contained supernatural powers, and with their acquisition, they would tap into them and become even more powerful and untouchable. The Dark Watchers, a group with a destructive agenda similar to that of the Children of the Nephilim, offered their services to assist them in pursuing total world domination. And always at the center was an insulated anonymous chairman wielding unfettered power.

"Their evilness and depravity gave rise to the Pure of Heart, warriors against the Children of the Nephilim and the Dark

Watchers. This group's mission was to defeat the Children of the Nephilim at all costs. They fought against their atrocities and pursued the location of those ancient treasures to hide them and keep them out of the hands of the Nephilim. Many Pure of Hearts died in their pursuit of preserving humanity and morality.

"Then, to my shock, Simon disclosed that he was the CEO of the Light Watchers, a worldwide clandestine organization that assisted the Pure of Heart in its mission. He managed all the financial and business affairs, coordinated operations, arranged extractions, and cataloged and secured the retrieved artworks. While Simon honored his country and Britain by fighting in the war, Chief Saunhac was the temporary CEO.

"I couldn't believe what he did next. He offered me the permanent position as CEO for the Light Watchers! He explained that he felt compelled to fight the evil agenda of the Chairman of the Children of the Nephilim. The Chairman, the son of a prominent family, was one of Simon's former university classmates. One night, while still at the university, Simon's classmate divulged in drunken hubris that his father was the current Chairman and that he was next in line. Realizing that he had violated his family's sacred secret, he grabbed Simon by his shirt, pulled him close, and snarled in his ear, "I will rip you from head to toe if you breathe a word of what I just told you." Simon did not doubt his threat. His classmate was a ruthless bully who had created and led a gang of young men recruited from on and off campus. They caused chaos and mayhem wherever they went. They threatened students, professors, and city people, creating an environment of fear. When the aging ruling patriarch of the Children of the Nephilim died, Simon's classmate stepped into his father's shoes as Chairman and took his evil reign from a university campus to the world.

"Simon knew his classmate was mean, but now, as the Chairman with massive power, he was a monster. With the assistance of the Dark Watchers, who had family members infiltrating pirates, mafias, and cartels, their evil potential was boundless.

"Simon believed that the only way to stop the Children of the Nephilim and their evil pursuits was to terminate the Chairman. He knew at the time his classmate blubbered his family secret that he could do nothing. Who would believe that his classmate was heir apparent to an evil secret organization? But now, he had the intelligence of the Light Watchers and the Pure of Heart and their active participation in fighting the Children of the Nephilim. Now, he had what he needed to chop off the head of the snake.

"Simon was torn. He was a husband. He was a soldier. He was the CEO of the Light Watchers. All of these were his priorities, but something had to go for him to pursue and eliminate the Chairman. He knew he had Dottie's support and assistance. His commitment to the military was nearly at its end. In his soul-searching, he accepted he could no longer fulfill the demands of the CEO position and engage in a full-time mission to bring the Chairman and his evil regime to an end.

"Simon discussed his decision to resign as the Light Watchers' CEO with Chief Saunhac and suggested he assume the position permanently. The Chief declined Simon's offer, explaining he needed to get back to his home and tend to tribal needs. But more importantly, it was not in his stars to hold the position. He'd seen in a vision that the young Canadian serving with Simon was the next CEO—ME!

"I was speechless. Looking like a gulping guppy, with my eyes bulging and my wordless lips flapping, I finally choked out my reservations. I was too young. I wasn't qualified. I had no experience.

Every excuse he countered. He then said, 'It is your destiny, Lumberjack. Chief Saunhac has seen it. He will assist you until you are ready to take the helm. The future of the Light Watchers is in your hands.'

"I had never heard of the Children of the Nephilim before my coffee break with Simon, but I believed every word he said. I could see in his eyes the urgency and the necessity of my acceptance. Facing the greatest fear I had ever experienced, I extended my hand and became the CEO of the Light Watchers.

"I held the position until last year when I turned the reins over to Bob. Like you, Han, my duty and my service were at a cost to my family. My son felt all his life that my job came before him. He thought I didn't care or love him when I loved him so much. I couldn't share with him the reason for my long absences because, as you know, that would have put my wife and child in danger. My priority was to keep them safe, so I stayed away and worked night and day, battling the Children of the Nephilim. Despite my precautions, the Dark Watchers identified my son and killed him and Cordy's mother. I worked so hard to protect the world but failed to protect my own son and daughter-in-law. I vowed I wouldn't fail Cordy." A tear ran down Bill's cheek.

Han reassured him, "You came through, Bill, when Cordy needed you most."

Bill mused, "Simon set us up for our futures, didn't he, Han? He sent you to search for the Keys of Life and me to lead the Light Watchers. And here we sit, drinking with his wife."

CHAPTER 10

WATER RESCUE

Dottie pretended to pout, "Bill, you touted how Simon saved you, but what about me? I saved you, too."

Laughing, Bill agreed, "Yes, you did, Dottie. I was going to bring that up when you and Han discussed his rescue, but your tale about Uriel distracted me. Yes, you rescued me under circumstances similar to Han's but without the dramatic assistance of an angel.

"I was on a reconnaissance mission for Operation Epsilon. T-Force had a target group of scientists they wanted to extract, but they needed to identify their exact location. It was my job to find them. I dressed like the locals to blend and move about without suspicion.

"One night, as I strolled nonchalantly down the street, a squad of Russian soldiers came toward me, conversing in their native language. I understood what they were saying since I was fluent in Russian. They were on the lookout for me. Their intel indicated an allied spy was in their vicinity. I walked on by, hoping that I would fly under their radar. Something about me caught their attention because, in Russian, one yelled, 'It's him! Get him!'

"Thankfully, before I engaged in any reconnaissance mission, I always scoped out multiple escape routes and had multiple escape plans prepared. Part of any escape plan was wearing layers of clothes to change my outer appearance if I had to be on the run.

"That preparation came in handy that night. I dashed and darted between side streets, shedding articles of clothing and dropping them in street cans as I passed. The Russians searched for a bare-headed man wearing a brown jacket and black horn-rimmed glasses. When I finally eluded them, I was down by the river, dressed in a black sweatshirt and a black ski cap, and no longer wearing glasses. I blended in with a group of East Germans putting their own escape plan into effect.

"Many East Germans didn't want to live under Soviet rule. They risked their lives to escape into the Kiel canals late at night, hiding in the frigid water and praying for rescue. Such was the intent of this group. When the time was right, they entered the water, not making a splash or a sound. I joined them.

"We were in the water for several hours waiting for rescue. Mothers consoled children and held them close to warm them as the water leached out our body temperature. I held onto an elderly gentleman who had weakened in strength. Finally, we heard your engine.

"I don't think I have ever been so happy to see a blond-haired woman as I was to see you that night."

Dottie chuckled, "I guided my Windy as close to you as possible. Between the two of us, we got all the refugees pulled out of the water onto my boat, and then we got the hell out of there."

"You and your Windy made quite a team! How did you become such an excellent sailor?"

"One of the few gifts I received from my nonattentive second husband, Alvan, was sailing skills. He was seldom home because business was his only priority. I complained about being lonely. Rather than cut his hours, he placated me by purchasing a small boat, thinking I could sail and fill my time. What a life-changer for me! Sailing gave me the peace and tranquility I didn't have at home. Sailing rescued me from boredom and loneliness. I never dreamed I would one day captain a yacht to rescue others from oppression and tyranny.

"Major Hebret, knew of my sailing skills. He assigned me to the team that assisted in the refugees' rescue. It was a dangerous assignment because we were sailing at night without lights. The canal was narrow and littered with rocks. It was tricky enough to maneuver during the day but nearly impossible at night.

"But, my yacht, Windy, was up for the challenge. She had the sleekest design, slicing through the water like a knife through butter. I equipped her with the best guidance and radio systems money could buy. She brought me great pleasure in peacetime and great honor in war. I was proud to captain her to aid those fleeing the horrors of war and the threat of oppressive regimes."

Bill lifted his glass in salute to Dottie, "Our two families owe you a great debt of gratitude. Without you, none of us would be here right now."

Taking a bow, Dottie replied, "Aw shucks, fellas. All in a day's work. My pleasure!"

CHAPTER 11

MONA

D ottie, didn't you say you assisted the Monuments Men?" inquired Bill.

"Yes, I did. We received an order from Winsty to send out a team to locate and retrieve treasures that the Germans had stolen from the Louvre. My primary task was to search all the records from when Germany invaded France, outlining the transport of the artwork and relics from the Louvre."

Bill choked on his water, "Do you mean Winston Churchill? You received a direct order from him?"

"Yes, I mean Winston Churchill, and no, I didn't receive the direct order; our team did. Winsty was a great art lover. He wanted all those treasures returned to their rightful place of honor, for public appreciation, not for an insane maniac's private hoard.

"Simon interviewed Albrecht Gaiswinkler, a man who escaped Austria and became a resistance fighter. He had located one of Hitler's secret hiding places, the Altaussee salt mines. Intelligence uncovered Germany's plan to blow up the salt mine and destroy all the treasures. Gaiswinkler and his team prevented that from happening.

"My records indicated many of the Louvre items could have ended up in those salt mines. The Monuments Men went to the salt mines and recovered 6,500 pieces of artwork and other treasures worth more than three point five billion dollars. One of those treasures was the *Mona Lisa*.

"There is much controversy about whether the *Mona Lisa* found at Altaussee was a replica or if it was the original. Hitler's greed for treasured artworks was well-known. With the German advancement into France, some have suggested that someone took proactive measures and had a copy made of the *Mona Lisa* to prevent Hitler from procuring the original and then hid the original at the Chateau d'Ambroise. It stayed hidden there until there was no more threat of German seizure. Others say that Hitler got his hands on the original, that it was the original *Mona Lisa* found in the salt mines.

"So, what say you, Bill? Did they find the original or a copy?"

Bill responded, "It's classified."

Preventing further discussion of the painting's authenticity, Bill suggested, "Hey, let's get a picture with Dottie so you can add it to your family album, Han. Dottie can have a memory of our trip into the past, and I'll have something to brag about to my boys. We don't get many opportunities to be in the company of beautiful blonds out on our fishing boats. They will be so jealous."

Bill withdrew his cell phone, "Give me that million-dollar Mona Lisa smile, Dottie."

Dottie's eyes twinkled, "Sure, Bill. Let me get in position. I have to be at the right angle."

Dottie struck a pose and imitated that famous smile. Bill snapped the picture. He checked it for clarity, and in astonishment, he handed the phone to Han to view the image. Dottie's likeness to the painting was so stunning that she could have been Mona Lisa herself.

Han stammered, "You look like you've done this before, Dottie. You look like you could be her."

Dottie smiled mischievously, "Perhaps."

Guiding them away from Mona Lisa's identity, Dottie asked them, "Did you know that Napoleon Bonaparte had possession of our lady, Mona? He had her in his and Josephine's bedroom, overlooking their bed.

"Oh, the stories Mona could tell, from her original creation to hanging in an emperor's boudoir, being a prisoner of war hidden in a salt mine, and finally returning to her home at the Louvre to thrill hearts with her beauty and mystery. Yes, our lady has quite the history."

CHAPTER 12

⟨∞⟩⟨∞⟩

THE ASTRONOMER

Han wondered aloud, "Dottie, isn't it believed Vermeer's *The Astronomer* joined our lady, Mona, in the salt mines?"

"Yes. At Hitler's order, the Germans seized the painting from the son of a Jewish banker's home and then stored it in the salt mines. Hitler desired it for its beauty and because he believed the painting contained secret messages."

Han interrupted, suggesting, "Let's move to the library, where it is more comfortable. I have a book there that highlights the works of the masters. We can look at the details in the painting as Dottie explains their significance to crazy, ole Hitler."

Han located the book and opened it to the section that analyzed the painting. He placed it on the library table so they could view it as one.

Dottie pointed to items in the picture. "Look at the stained-glass window and how the light subtly infuses the room but also focuses on the globe. Hitler may have thought that light endowed the painting with supernatural power. Now, notice what else Vermeer included. The globe is a rendering of the night sky, a nod to the scientist's profession. The book on the table references the relationship between the study of astronomy and geography, and it's opened to Book III. This section encourages the astronomer to turn to God for direction. Hitler would not have sought God's direction because he was an atheist and considered himself a god, but he may have seen that reference as further proof of its supernatural power. And Han, note the painting on the wall."

"Oh my gosh. It's a painting titled, *Finding of Moses.*"

Flipping pages and settling on one, he summarized, "The profile for the Moses painting says it may symbolize knowledge and science. That's something Hitler would crave."

Han looked at Dottie, "So, how did the painting end up under a bed in Austria?"

Dottie shared, "Simon told me that the Chairman of the Children of the Nephilim and Hitler were practically clones of each other. They both desired artworks they deemed to be of the supernatural realm to increase their own world power. In their narcissism, they felt they were the only ones who deserved to live with treasured beauty surrounding them. So, like Hitler, the Chairman stole by proxy whatever he desired, even at the cost of life.

"Simon believed the Chairman had one of his agents, Victor Mahlov, infiltrate the German security team, steal the Vermeer from Hitler's hoard, and then hide it in the farmhouse. It was quite a coup for the Chairman to acquire one of Hitler's treasures right from under his nose.

"Simon also believed that the soldiers you confronted in the farmhouse, Bill, were actually Nephilim agents impersonating

Russian soldiers. Part of the Nephilim playbook was to distract and deflect."

"Still is," interjected Bill.

Dottie continued, "If anything went wrong in the plan, such as the capture or the death of the impersonators, then the blame would fall on Russia, and no one would be the wiser of the actual responsible party."

There was a sudden change in Dottie's tone. She was no longer a storyteller but now a woman who was angry and hurting. "Securing this painting and pursuing the Chairman got my Simon killed!"

CHAPTER 13

LOVE LOST

W hat???" thundered Bill and Han simultaneously.

"Take a seat, boys, and I'll tell you the rest."

Dottie began to wander the room as she resumed her story.

"Simon did not easily relinquish his CEO position to you, Bill. We spent many a night discussing his plans. He knew what the Chairman was capable of, his art of deception, and his expertise in keeping himself insulated from exposure. He understood his thirst for power at all costs. He feared the Chairman would use the newly discovered nuclear technology as a threat to bend the other world powers to his bidding or as a weapon to terminate those countries who opposed him. That was the tipping point. He could no longer stay in the background. It was time to pursue the elusive Chairman aggressively.

"As our term with the military was ending, MI6 offered us positions in the organization to work as a team or individually, as missions required. Simon saw this as an opportunity to kill two birds with one stone. We could continue to serve our adopted country and at the same time have more freedom to pursue the Chairman.

"So, he turned over the Light Watchers to you, Bill. We completed our time with the military and then joined MI6. While honoring our assignments for MI6, Simon became a one-person army relentlessly searching for the Chairman, spending every free moment analyzing data and intelligence and pursuing any reasonable lead. I assisted him as much as possible. From the intel, we were closing in on the Chairman's location.

"After a time, exhaustion threatened to derail us. We took no break between finishing the military and beginning our time with MI6. Added to that, we were spending all of our personal time searching for the Chairman. The physical and mental energy that all of this required took its toll. We realized we needed a respite from our official and personal responsibilities to rejuvenate and regroup. We requested a short holiday, and MI6 greenlighted it.

"We loaded up Windy and set sail for our long-overdue weekend. We were having a grand time. Even though it was a holiday, we remained vigilant. To an observer, we sailed aimlessly, but we always knew our exact location. On deck, curious eyes witnessed two young lovebirds who couldn't keep their hands off each other. Anyone watching saw a couple absorbed in each other, but we were aware of our surroundings the entire time.

"On a peaceful afternoon, Simon desired a little afternoon delight. I snuggled under the blanket with him, and we gave any watcher an eyeful. We rocked our boat back and forth, causing wave surges that nearly capsized us. We remained below deck most of the afternoon.

"After a light supper, Simon leisurely strolled on deck, satiated from an afternoon of love and enjoying the setting sun. I quickly tidied the galley to join him when I heard shots. I grabbed the machine gun Simon left by the door and bounded up the ladder.

"Two boats whirled around us, spraying bullets. Splinters of wood erupted into the air. Windows shattered, sending shards everywhere. I tossed the gun to Simon, and he returned fire. He yelled at me that he recognized our assailants as Mahlov's men, the Chairman's right-hand man.

"I pushed to full throttle and propelled us away while sending out a mayday notifying anyone who heard me that the Windy was under attack from pirates and needed immediate assistance.

"I went into defensive mode, trying to escape the assassins. Then, one shot rang loud. I'll never forget that sound. Everything went into slow motion as I watched my darling Simon crumple to the deck. I couldn't stop the boat to aid him. I had to keep going to get away. Like a robot, I shifted the gears and zig-zagged through the water, keeping the enemy at bay.

"As I began to lose hope, I heard the roar of an airplane engine. A spitfire came zooming in, firing machine guns at our attackers, keeping them busy so I could pull away. When I was clear, the pilot increased the deluge of bullets, piercing their vessels and gas tanks. Within moments, both boats exploded. There was nothing left but char and debris.

"Then a voice came over the radio, 'This is Kora, the pilot. I saw the firestorm from the air and then recognized Windy. Threat eliminated. I'm calling in for more support.'

"I couldn't believe it was my Attagirl pal who had come to our rescue. Sobbing, I responded, 'Kora, it's Dirty Dottie. Thank you for your assistance. Simon took a shot to the chest. I fear he's bleeding out. Call for a medical team.'

"I ran to Simon and kneeled beside him. Blood pooled on the

deck floor. I had seen injuries like this before. I knew he was dying, but I had to try to save him. I pressed my hands against the wound, but no matter how much pressure I applied, I couldn't slow the bleeding.

"Simon struggled as he whispered, 'I love you, Dottie. You have always made me very happy. Tell Bill and Han I found joy.'

"I stroked his thick hair and gazed into his dimming eyes. 'Simon, I love you. You and I have shared a love beyond measure. You will always be in my heart. I'll miss you.' I leaned over and kissed his lips one last time.

"In a weak voice, he assured me, 'I'll be waiting for you, Dottie.'

"He stopped breathing, and his eyes fixed on the pink evening sky."

Spent from her story, Dottie collapsed onto the sofa with tears streaming down her cheeks as she mourned once again for love lost.

CHAPTER 14

MONIQUE

They all sat in silence for a few moments. Without a word exchanged, Bill moved beside Dottie and held her hand in comfort. Han quietly exited the library and returned with freshened glasses of water and a tissue box. He gently asked Dottie, "Would you like something stronger than this, or would you like to call it a night? Aziza always has a guest room prepared."

Drying her eyes, Dottie took the glass Han offered. "Thank you, the water is fine. If you two old guys would indulge me a bit longer, I need to tell you the rest. I believe you'll find that Simon's story has a satisfactory ending and maybe will lessen our grief."

Han looked sorrowfully at Dottie, "I received a message that Simon had been killed, but there were no details."

Bill concurred, "I received the same message."

"MI6 didn't know of Simon's work regarding the Chairman, so I created a cover story to explain what happened and how Simon knew who attacked us. I reported to MI6 and the authorities that pirates surrounded us to steal the yacht and kill Simon. As piracy had become an issue, both organizations accepted the explanation and did not pursue it further. I further explained that Simon recognized the attackers as Mahlov's men because they were part of one of the smuggling rings he had been tracking during the war. Since it appeared that we were a targeted hit, MI6 was concerned there was a mole who leaked our location. To launch their inside investigation, MI6 decided to keep the details regarding Simon's death minimal. That's why you received the simple statement of death.

"I continued to work for MI6 as an individual operative. I utilized my extensive language skills and ability to become a chameleon to gain vital intelligence and identify potential threats to our country. My commitment to MI6 was always my priority, but I never stopped looking and listening for information regarding Mahlov.

"MI6 eventually identified the mole, unaware she was one of the Chairman's plants. After several hours of grueling interrogation, she finally broke and betrayed Mahlov, confirming his responsibility for the hit on Simon. She also described how Mahlov planned to assassinate Winston Churchill and arrange it so the Russians appeared responsible. The goal was to create world chaos and perhaps another world war. What she wouldn't or couldn't tell us was who ordered Mahlov to commit these crimes.

"MI6 soon discovered that Mahlov was living it up in Monte Carlo, feeding his addictions to gambling, vodka, and women. Now it was time to pay, oops, I mean play.

"I traveled to Monte Carlo and entered his hotel with flaming red hair, a round middle, and orthotic shoes, registering as Muriel Smith. Once in my room, I exchanged the red wig for a salt-and-pepper wig, changed into a housekeeping uniform MI6 had provided, and slipped in an orthodontic appliance to change my facial appearance. I exited the room and moved to the towel cart casually left by my door. For all appearances, an aging floor maid was completing her daily assignment.

"I arrived at Mahlov's room and, in a sing-song voice, announced myself as housekeeping. As no one answered, I used a pass key and let myself in. I hastily unburied the go-bag concealed in the pile of towels and searched the immense ornate room for a hidey hole. Staged on a broad-based pedestal was a statue of an open-winged red-haired angel. I pulled on a pair of gloves, removed the porcelain statue, and tipped the heavy base. Discovering it to be hollow, I crammed my bag inside. I repositioned the base and returned the statue to its place of honor. I made certain the room was tidy and that I had not left any evidence of my presence. Stuffing the gloves into the pocket of my uniform, I gave my guardian angel a wink in gratitude and pushed the cart back to my room. I grabbed another stack of towels and pushed the door open, calling out, 'Housekeeping' as I strode in.

"Later in the evening, disguised as Muriel, I left the room and went to the casino. Seated at the poker table, tossing back his vodka, my red hair caught Mahlov's eye, but my round figure and apparent age withered his interest. I wiggled on by him and headed to the ladies' room.

"A bit later, I exited the restroom as a blond-haired uniformed hotel attendant and made my way to the rear of the hotel. I picked through a clothes rack, selected a black garment bag, and entered Monique's dressing room.

"An hour later, Monique left her room and proceeded to the stage for her debut performance.

"Mahlov nearly tumbled out of his chair as the black-haired beauty with ruby-red lips floated across the stage. The vision before him adorned a strapless, black sequined gown with a red satin cummerbund accenting her hourglass figure.

"The music swelled, and she began to sing. Her voice captivated every man's heart. They only had eyes for her. As the song progressed, Monique made eye contact with Mahlov. Never breaking that contact, she moved into the audience, singing her song, occasionally smoothing her hand through an adoring man's hair, and slowly approached Mahlov. She sat on his lap and stroked his face as she finished the final verse.

"He hungrily grabbed Monique and growled, 'I must have you!'

"Monique leaned into him, licked the side of his face, and purred, 'And you will. I will join you when I finish my set.'

"Monique broke many a heart that night as she only had eyes for the big man at the poker table. Finishing the set, she slipped on a pair of elbow-length, red opera gloves and returned to the poker table.

"Sweeping around him, aerating her sensual perfume, Monique asked him, 'Was my performance satisfying, Monsieur?'

"Mahlov barked, 'Not nearly. I demand another private performance from you! In my room! Now!'

"Monique slinked before him and leaned in, 'But of course, Monsieur. I wish only for your pleasure.'

"Mahlov cashed in his chips and, with restraint, wrapped his arm around Monique's waist, and escorted her out of the casino, bodyguards in tow.

"Upon arriving at Mahlov's suite, he ordered the bodyguards to check his room and affirm its safety and privacy. Giving the all-clear, they returned to the hall to stand guard. Mahlov slammed the door after them and bolted the lock.

"Once in the room, Mahlov yanked Monique in for a scorching kiss. 'I want you now! Strip!'

"Monique slipped her arms around his neck and pouted, 'But, Monsieur, I have had a long night. Singing has made me so thirsty. Let us have a drink before I perform for you. You go to the bedroom and prepare for me. I will fix your cocktail just as you like and serve you in bed like a king. Then I will dance for you, the Dance of the Seven Veils.

Mahlov never suspected he was a fly entering the black widow's web. As he impatiently waited in the bedroom, Monique concocted his favorite cocktail with a little something extra. She opened the locket around her neck and gently shook out a small vial. She broke it open and sprinkled its contents into Mahlov's glass. Giving it a final stir and adding his favored lime, she filled a matching short tumbler with water and added a lemon slice. Placing both on a gold tray, she sashayed into the bedroom.

"Naked, Mahlov reclined on the bed. There was no question to his desire. Monique admired him with great appreciation and then handed him his glass. 'Drink, Monsieur. I promise it will begin your pleasure.'

"She moved away from the bed, her hips swaying side to side. She turned around and encouraged him to finish his drink. His reward would be her dance and then his fulfillment. As she slowly slid each glove down her arms, she danced to music no one could hear and let the gloves flow across her body, caressing her seductive curves.

"Once he finished his drink, Monique returned to the bed and locked eyes with him. She wrapped her hands around his wrists to hold him in place and leaned down to kiss him, but just before their lips met, she paused and whispered, 'Your sins have come to roost, Mahlov. Remember the murder and mayhem you have committed. Remember the day you assassinated Simon Cross. May he be your final thoughts as you take your last breath.'

"As his eyes filled with horrified understanding, excruciating pain surged through his chest, crushing the breath from his lungs. In a few moments, he was no more.

"Monique grabbed the glasses, went to the kitchenette, and washed them, ensuring she left no fingerprints. Slipping her gloves back on, she returned the glasses and the tray to their place on the bar. She rushed to the pedestal, retrieved her go-bag, and repositioned the base and the angel. She kicked off her heels, stripped out of her gloves and gown, and pulled an all-black cat-suit from the bag. She yanked off her wig and slithered into the catsuit. She covered her head and face with a full-face ski mask, tugged on black, soft-soled boots, and donned black cotton gloves. Lastly, she extracted the remaining item in her go-bag, a miniature camera. With her costume change complete, she stuffed the performance clothes into the now-empty bag, grabbed the camera, and dashed into the bedroom.

"Leaning against the desk was Mahlov's locked briefcase. It took Monique only a moment to open it and expose a cache of valuable information. A quick perusal of the top files outlined the assassination plots of Churchill and other perceived threats to the Chairman. At the bottom of the pile was a dossier on Simon Cross.

"Monique carefully examined the information it contained. An intelligence report revealed Simon to be a Light Watcher. Next was a summary of complaints from the Chairman regarding Simon's interference with his acquisition of *The Astronomer* and his grow-ing fear that Simon was homing in on him. If the Chairman's greedy, paranoid rants weren't enough to order Simon's death, the following document sealed his fate. In her hands, Monique held Simon's astrological star birth chart. The Chairman used these charts to identify Pure of Hearts. If the stars aligned to verify the individual as a Pure of Heart, the Chairman ordered their immediate execution. Simon's chart confirmed he was indeed a Pure of Heart. With shaking hands, Monique read the final two documents—the assassination order for Simon Cross and the follow-up report detailing his murder.

"Taking a calming breath, Monique refocused and resumed her mission. She spread the files out individually and snapped pictures of each document that detailed the threats to national security. She left those referencing Simon's murder hidden at the bottom of the briefcase and hidden in her heart. Her assignment completed, she returned everything to Mahlov's traitorous box, relocked it, and put it back beside the desk. Making sure everything was as it was when she and Mahlov entered the room, she grabbed her go-bag, saluted the red-haired angel, turned off the lights, and exited via the fire escape.

"Monique silently raced through the shadows to the dock, boarded a boat, and quietly sailed away in the darkness."

In awe, Bill said, "You killed Victor Mahlov."

In a French accent, Dottie replied innocently, "Oh no, Monsieur, not Dottie nor Monique. It was a heart attack."

CHAPTER 15

~~~

SURPRISE TWICE

Han massaged his forehead and contemplated aloud, "Simon's last words, 'I found joy,' have me thinking, Bill."

"What perplexes you? I also find Simon's message to Dottie puzzling. Of course, he found joy with you, Dottie, but why would he want us to know that? I think you're correct, Han. There has to be more to his final statement than the literal words."

Dottie soberly added, "I wondered then why it was essential for Simon to share those words with you. We had not seen you since we finished our military responsibilities and assignments. Why would you care if Simon and I were happy together? I agree. His message has to have more meaning than his declaration of love for me."

"Wait a minute!" exclaimed Bill. "I just remembered something. Simon told me that the Vermeer painting wasn't the only treasure the Chairman craved. He had his tentacles out to locate and steal another relic. Simon was monitoring Light Watchers' intelligence to see if he could determine the item and acquire it before the Chairman.

"Han, would you log onto your computer for me? We weren't computerized when I started as CEO, but once we were, we scanned a lot of the hard copy information into electronic files. I can still access the Light Watchers' system. I'll see if there is a record of Simon's intelligence history.

"Ah, here it is, a file dedicated to Simon Cross." Bill carefully perused the information. "I don't believe it! He was looking for Joyeuse, Charlemagne's battle sword! From the information in this file, I think he was telling us he found Charlemagne's sword, Joy, not sharing how he felt about Dottie.

"It's within reason that the Chairman would covet the sword. Legend has it that the sword absorbed strength and power from each of its conquests, making any wielder greater than his enemy, guaranteeing victory. It is easy to see how the Chairman might have believed he would be invincible if he possessed the sword."

While Bill continued to read the electronic report, Han researched the sword in one of his books. He turned the book to Dottie and Bill and pointed to a picture of the relic and a synopsis of its history and legend.

Dottie read the caption under the sword and wondered, "But, it says here that the sword is in the Louvre."

Han nodded in agreement and said, "Yes, but some believe that Charlemagne had two swords: his battle sword, Joyeuse, and a sword he used for ceremonies. Those who support the two-sword theory propose the sword in the Louvre is Charlemagne's ceremonial sword, used in coronations, not Joyeuse, his actual battle sword."

Han continued reading, "*The Song of Roland* describes the

battle sword of Charlemagne as magical. When wielded in warfare, it shone so bright it blinded Charlemagne's enemy.

"When resting at the king's side, the light radiated from it, changing color thirty times a day. It has come to symbolize power and authority.

"Could it be he actually found Joyeuse?"

Dottie stated, "Whatever Simon found, it was significant. If he were trying to keep it out of the hands of the Chairman, his first choice would have been to get it to the Light Watchers headquarters for Chief Saunhac to hide it in one of their secret places. There would have been no need to tell me or anyone else he found it.

"He must not have been able to get it to the Light Watchers, so he hid it somewhere, and his message was a subtle way to tell us to find it. But how do we know where to look? His assignments took him all over Europe and Canada."

Snapping his fingers in realization, Bill cried enthusiastically, "I got it! I bet he hid it on the old Cross property!"

"What property?" Dottie asked incredulously. "I know nothing of Simon's background before we were married other than his affiliation with the Light Watchers. I'm not even sure his parents knew we were married. When we joined MI6, he arranged to have his background erased and recreated so that he had no family, and his birthplace was England, not Canada. I understood the extreme measures he took to protect his parents from repercussions. We were in a dangerous business of national espionage and trying to take down a shadow government.

"He went home for an occasional visit. I never asked where home was to honor and maintain his secrecy, but I knew how he protected his identity and destination. Disguised, he left in the dark of night and traveled a circuitous route. No matter what time of day he landed, he never arrived at his parents' until after dark. He would have a driver drop him off at a different pub each time, and then he would walk the rest of the way like a phantom through dark alleys and the woods. If anyone was watching, they never saw him leave the pub nor enter his home. He returned to England in the same covert manner. It might have been in one of those few visits that he journeyed with the sword and hid it."

"Well, Dottie and Han, here is the second surprise for the evening. I didn't know until after Chief Saunhac died that the Cross family lived down the road from him. The Saunhac property and the Cross property back up to each other. Simon grew up under the chief's tutelage."

"Bloody hell, you're kidding me, Bill!"

"No, Dottie. It's true. Cordy is Chief Saunhac's only heir. Bob and I assisted her in wading through his complex will. The chief was thorough, but it took time to get through it all. One thing he left was a detailed journal describing his close relationship with the Cross family. We knew the journal had to have some significance because the chief didn't write without a purpose, but we couldn't figure it out. It seemed like a simple story of friendship when we first read it, so we set it aside as a sweet anecdote. But now, knowing what we do, the chief probably had a vision about this precise moment and left the journal to assist us.

"According to the journal, Chief Saunhac was friends with the Cross family, well mostly friends with Mrs. Cross and her young son. Mr. Cross made friends with no one as he hung on to his life-long anger and resentment.

"Life in the Cross household was difficult. Mr. Cross was narrow-minded and a harsh disciplinarian. He and Simon were polar opposites, which caused conflict between them. Mr. Cross felt all loyalty was to home and family. However, Simon had a broader view of the world and a desire to serve a greater good beyond hearth and home.

"Occasionally, Simon would wander over for a visit with the chief. They would talk about everyday life, silly things, and dreams. The chief taught him how to carve, enjoy and appreciate nature, and be at peace in his father's hostile environment. The boy and Chief Saunhac became close as time passed, forging a special bond. Then, the chief had a vision that revealed Simon was a Pure of Heart.

"Signaled by the spirits that the time was right, Chief Saunhac explained the battle between the Children of the Nephilim and the Pure of Heart. He shared with Simon his vision regarding Simon's identity and his responsibility if he accepted it.

"Simon always felt destined to do something outside their small town. He just wasn't sure what that was. Now he knew. He embraced it with one-hundred percent commitment, always in pursuit of protecting Pure of Heart treasures and eventually becoming the Light Watchers' CEO. It also influenced his decision to join the military.

"Mr. Cross was outraged when Simon told him his plans. He wanted Simon to pursue post-graduate education and become a professor, but Simon felt called to aid the Allied forces. He enlisted and quickly advanced up the ranks. To make matters worse between father and son, the military assigned Simon to a post in England. Mr. Cross accused him of abandoning his family and threatened to disinherit him.

"It was a lonely life for Mrs. Cross after Simon deployed. She understood his need to serve and was proud of him, but the joy and hope he once brought to their home were gone. All that remained was Mr. Cross's bitterness, which, like poison, destroyed his heart. He succumbed to a heart attack, leaving Mrs. Cross totally alone. So, as her young son had once done, she wandered over many an afternoon and visited with the chief, seeking solace and understanding, becoming close friends.

"Before she passed, Mrs. Cross bequeathed all her property and possessions to Chief Saunhac. Now, since his death, all that belongs to Cordy and Ash. We've discussed what action to take but haven't made any decisions. We haven't touched anything in the house. Everything is still in place exactly as when Mrs. Cross lived there. I think......."

"Han! Han!" Trembling, Aziza flew into the library on the verge of hysteria.

Responding to her fear, Han rushed to her, enveloped her in his arms, and asked, "What's wrong, darling? Are the twins all right?"

Holding onto Han's arms tightly, Aziza leaned back and stared into his eyes. Steadied by the comfort and reassurance she saw there, she haltingly explained, "A terrifying vision woke me. We are in imminent danger. A man with murderous intentions lurks nearby. The blackness of evil surrounds him. His heart beats, but it is dead. I see him clearly, Han."

"Take a breath and tell us what you see, honey."

"He is bald. Reptilian eyes. Average in height but stocky in build. A large, purple birthmark on his right cheek. Arrogant. He carries a weapon. He's in search of something of great value. I can't see what it is, but he plans to kill us all when he finds it. He is watching." Aziza swooned from the intensity of the vision and started to crumble.

Han scooped her up before she hit the floor and tenderly carried her quaking body to the sofa. Dottie covered her with a blanket, and Bill handed her a water glass from the table.

"Hells bells and monkey tails!" Dottie exclaimed. "Aziza's description fits the man sitting beside me on the plane to a tee. He was bald, had a stocky build, and had that birthmark. In a pompous, scholarly manner, he pontificated on all sorts of antiquities and legends. I thought he was attempting to impress me with his knowledge. I never considered he may have been pumping me for information. When I entertained him in my Dirty Dottie fashion, he didn't respond to my sexy jokes and ended the conversation, turning his nose up as if I offended him, stuffy old goat. It never occurred to me that he was following me. I have no idea who this clown is, but we need to find out. I'm sorry, Aziza, if I brought danger to your door."

Bill knelt before Aziza and took her hands, "Aziza, I think the three of us know what this is about. We have been rehashing some of our experiences protecting the Pure of Heart treasures during World War II. We've made startling discoveries about how our paths intersected in ways we never realized. Tonight, we think we answered a mystery Dottie has been carrying with her for a long time. If we're correct, that explains the man in your vision. We don't know who he is, but we have an idea of what he is after.

"Han and Dottie, I think we better check this out tonight. I was going to suggest we investigate the Cross property in the morning, but with this information, we better go now, in the secret of darkness.

"Aziza, we'll have to leave the house. Ash and Cordy are here. They'll keep you safe."

Removing the blanket and assisting Aziza to her feet, Han assured her, "I'll help you back to bed and alert Ash. It will take some doing, but I will convince him he must remain here with you and the twins."

Han anticipated a fight with Ash but never dreamed he would face off with Aziza and Cordy, too. Aziza refused to go to bed and argued with him as he changed into black clothes and retrieved a backpack. Ash and Cordy refused to stay in bed, with Ash protesting as they all trailed into the library, "I don't like this. I want to go with you. You might need me."

"Son, I need you more here to protect what is most precious to me: your mother, your siblings, you, and our Cordy."

Ash begrudgingly acquiesced, "OK. I'll be waiting right here. But, for the record, I hate this! You better come back in one piece!"

Cordy interjected, "We'll be right here! You three, be careful. You're all that we have!" Cordy hugged each one.

"I'll be right back, boys. I need five minutes." Dottie snatched up her carry-on bag and dashed to the powder room. To her word, five minutes later, she emerged wearing a skin-tight black catsuit and black tennis shoes, her hair stuffed in a black skull cap.

Ash lustily whispered to Cordy, "You have got to get one of those suits so I can rip it off you with my teeth." Cordy jabbed him in the ribs, knocking the wind out of him.

Han and Bill goggled at Dottie's transformation, prompting her to redirect their attention, "Ready, boys?"

Gathering their wits, they grabbed their backpacks containing anticipated tools and buckled holsters around their waists.

After another round of hugs, Han led them to a secret exit at the back of the house, and they walked out into the darkness.

CHAPTER 16

JOSEF VON KRUEGER

The Chairman of the Children of the Nephilim became incensed when Hitler acquired the Spear of Destiny. He now had another relic that could empower him for world domination. That could not happen! Only the Chairman was destined for that position!

To outdo Hitler, the Chairman made it his quest to locate and apprehend another sword imbued with magical powers, Charlemagne's battle sword, Joyeuse. The power of that treasure would further the Chairman's empire. He would be the Charlemagne of his time! He would be the emperor of the world!

This would require a team devoted to its search and acquisition. The Chairman summoned his head advisor to acquire a list of recommendations to staff the unit.

At the top of the list was a young man named Josef von Krueger. He was a first-year student at the University of Kiel studying art history. His knowledge of art in general and his expertise in medieval art and artifacts set him apart from his peers and most of his professors. He wasn't there for education. He knew what he needed to know, but he required the credentials of a university degree. He'd play the game until he got what he desired: entrance into museums and wealthy private owners. Then, he would build his own personal collection at no cost to him.

The Chairman conducted the interview as a private collector to maintain his anonymity. He would not announce his identity until he was confident of von Krueger's allegiance. He explained to von Krueger that he desired to increase his collection. He needed someone to research and locate those pieces and then acquire them. Von Krueger saw through the subterfuge and understood that his potential employer desired the acquisitions through larcenous means. After all, like recognized like.

Von Krueger opened his briefcase and withdrew a rolled canvas. He unfurled it to display Vermeer's *The Astronomer*. Stunned, the collector looked at von Krueger and demanded, "I desire this painting. How did you acquire it?"

"I didn't," replied von Krueger. "I painted it. This is what I can do for you. I can paint forgeries or outsource to a talented team at my disposal. I can replace originals with reproductions when we locate what you desire. No one will be the wiser.

"I can be your assistant or representative for public or private acquisitions to increase your collection and advance your reputation within the art world. All of this I can do for you, and more, as situations require."

The two settled on a trial period. Before the private collector revealed his real desire, he requested his new employee to acquire small, inconsequential treasures to guarantee he could do what he promised. Von Krueger was true to his word. He obtained all of the items by legal or illegal means. Convinced of von Krueger's loyalty and skill, the private collector invited him to join him for dinner in his home.

After they completed their decadent meal, the collector led von Krueger to his opulent office. He motioned for von Krueger to take the chair before the immense, gold-filigreed desk while he moved to the throne behind it. Settled, he looked straight into von Krueger's eyes. Von Krueger no longer saw the art-hungry collector. What he saw was pure, unadulterated evil. That should have frightened him, but instead, it thrilled him.

His host began, "I have had you vetted."

"I assumed you would, Sir. This does not offend me, nor does it threaten me. Someone in your position would want to make sure that I am who I say I am and can do what I say I can do. You could not be this successful if you weren't cautious. I am sure you found that I am precisely the person I said I am, and I genuinely have the skill set to meet your needs."

"If I continue this discussion with you, I own you. You serve no one else. You work for no one else. You do exactly as I tell you, no questions asked. You will be fairly compensated, but if you betray me, I will kill you."

"I understand, Sir. I also understand that I can't say no. If I do, you will kill me because you have confided too much in your offer. Thankfully for you and me, I desire this position. I agree to your terms. I am here to serve you."

"Good! I hated the idea of eliminating your mind and your skill. I think we will make a good team. Let me give you a bit of background about our organization and who I really am.

"To the world, I am a wealthy antiquities and art collector. Behind closed doors, I am the Chairman of a shadow government called the

Children of the Nephilim. We have been in existence since the beginning of time. With power taken from Pure of Heart treasures, our goal is to obtain world dominion. We have no scruples. We take what we want and need. We infiltrate governments to gain intelligence and manipulate them to our advantage. We steal their art, science, and technology for our gain. Right now, Hitler is my nemesis, both in his quest to be the ruler of the world and in the artwork he is obtaining. This is where I require you and your skills.

"I've already told you that I desire *The Astronomer* by Vermeer. Get it for me! Any means necessary.

"However, my greatest desire is Charlemagne's battle sword, Joyeuse. Find it! Its power will advance me beyond Hitler!"

"Yes sir! I will start my research for the painting and the sword immediately."

Von Krueger searched for the painting for the entire duration of the war. He knew Hitler had it but couldn't locate it. Once allied teams discovered it in one of Hitler's secret bunkers and planned to return it to the family, von Krueger saw a way to intercept it and finally acquire it for the Chairman. It would require a Nephilim team to put the plan into action. The Chairman assigned his man Mahlov.

Together, von Krueger and Mahlov planned the mission. Mahlov's men would appear as Russian soldiers and steal the painting. They would then store it in an abandoned farmhouse in Austria. Von Krueger would exchange the original for his reproduction. The family would receive the copy, and the Chairman would add the original to his secret treasure room. However, Simon Cross and his minion, Bill Mc Dermott, foiled their plan.

The Chairman was furious at the loss of the painting. Thankfully for von Krueger and Mahlov, the Chairman attributed the failure to Simon Cross, not them. He ordered Mahlov to find Cross and kill him.

After the loss of *The Astronomer*, von Krueger intensified his search for Charlemagne's battle sword. He would think he was close and then hit a dead end. It became evident that Simon Cross also hunted for the sword. Then, all leads stopped, and there was no evidence that Cross pursued the treasure any longer. Had he located it and hidden it away?

Even though he kept coming up cold, Von Krueger persevered in his search for the sword. The Chairman endlessly complained about his lack of progress. Knowing he would never give up on his desire to possess the sword and knowing a dissatisfied Chairman usually led to a death sentence, von Krueger acquired meaningless baubles and treasures to distract him and dangled false leads regarding the sword to appease him. He continued to feed the Chairman's lust for the sword and remind him that once acquired, it would move him closer to his goal of world dominion. His patience would pay off.

No one could predict the impact the search for the sword would have on von Krueger. He became obsessed with the legend of the sword's power, driving him to visions of grandeur. In his greed and narcissism, he deemed he had all the qualities and skills necessary to run an empire. Why shouldn't he be the Chairman?

He would use the Children of the Nephilim resources and continue to search for the sword, but when he found it, he would use its power to overthrow the Chairman and his family. He would proclaim himself as the Chairman! He would reign when the moment was right.

After years of searching, bobbing, and weaving to distract the Chairman from his lack of progress, von Krueger finally had a break, all because his wife made him sit through an insufferable dinner theater on a riverboat.

They were vacationing in Memphis as his wife was a long-time fan of Elvis Presley and desired to tour Graceland and do all the touristy things there. She saw a flyer for a riverboat dinner cruise and insisted they book a table. He hated the very idea but obliged his wife. Then Atropa Nightshade came onto the stage. He never imagined that someone resembling Dottie Cross would be the lead performer. If it was Dottie, she must have had an excellent plastic surgeon because this woman looked just like the pictures he had seen in the late 1940s.

Von Krueger excused himself and went to the strolling deck. He pretended to smoke a cigarette so no one would question why a lone man was out there. He withdrew his cell phone and called the Nephilim mole they currently had assigned to MI6. He ordered him to do a deep search on Dottie Cross going back to 1945.

As the cigarette burned down, von Krueger gazed into the black water. His memories drifted to 1945 and the killing of Simon Cross. The tart assigned by the Chairman to the MI6 office reported that the married couple would be vacationing at sea. She provided their coordinates and pictures of them and their sailing vessel. Von Krueger suggested they capture Simon and bring him to Nephilim headquarters for interrogation regarding the sword. But the Chairman was in a blood-red rage. Simon frightened and offended him. His former classmate knew his true identity and had intercepted one of his heart's desires, the Vermeer painting. No reason would sway him. The Chairman had only one course: kill Simon Cross. Mahlov, never thinking beyond the orders of the Chairman, carried out his duty without question or hesitation.

Von Krueger's thoughts tumbled back to the present with the vibration of his cell phone. His mole reported that researching MI6 archives had identified an operative named Dottie Cross, who worked in the late 1940s, but her information ended there. There were other Dotties with different last names through the years, but none resembled the picture associated with Dottie Cross. Von Krueger ordered him to investigate the other Dotties' dossiers and determine if any information connected to the Dottie Cross of 1945.

Von Krueger then called his research and intelligence team and ordered a records search for the owner of the riverboat. They reported that Big Jim Black Enterprises owned it—no mention of a 'Dottie' anywhere in titles or licenses.

He put in another call to an elite Dark Watchers surveillance team. He gave them the information as he knew it and ordered 24/7 surveillance using any resource or equipment necessary to determine her identity.

His intuition told him that the woman on the stage was Dottie Cross. He returned to the playhouse, convinced the sword would soon be in his hand.

CHAPTER 17

WAITING AND WATCHING

Von Krueger's team followed Dottie from the airport to the hotel, informing him of her whereabouts. He rented a car, drove to her location, and began surveillance. A few hours later, she left the hotel and boarded a taxicab. The driver drove at a breakneck speed and handled the twists and turns like a pro. Tailing him had been a challenge as he struggled to keep up without blowing his cover or drawing attention from the other drivers. But he managed. Once Dottie entered the house, von Krueger searched out his hiding place. He contacted his intelligence team and provided the address. They reported that the residence belonged to Cordy von Lettow, great-granddaughter of Chief Saunhac.

"Isn't that interesting? Chief Saunhac is very famous in our war with the Pure of Heart. I must be in the right place."

Keeping a watchful eye on the house, von Krueger considered how things fell into place for him. His surveillance team had difficulty gathering information because Dottie had jammers. That in itself made him believe she was indeed the mysterious Dottie Cross. She conducted all of her business under her stage name, Atropa Nightshade. Her background withstood most deep background checks, but his team of superb experts determined she was using an assumed identity. Then, the best coincidence. His MI6 mole was in the office when Dottie called to notify her boss that she was taking a little vacation to Nova Scotia. The mole informed him immediately.

Using a plant in Dottie's housekeeping staff, he ascertained her flight arrangements. After all, he could create flawless credentials, too.

He booked the same flight and paid extra for a seat assignment next to her. It cost him a pretty penny, but it was worth it. He assumed he would converse with a serious-minded, educated woman who might give him information about the sword. Instead, he found her to be a bubblehead and tiresome with her oversexed innuendoes. How could she have such an illustrious reputation? She had to have connections or, more than likely, slept her way to get into the high position she had at MI6. No matter. She didn't have to be intelligent or a lady to lead him to Joyeuse.

Von Krueger remained in his hiding place all afternoon, conducting surveillance. When darkness shrouded the house, he switched to a thermal imaging camera to monitor the movement of those inside. Around midnight, there was a flurry that caught his attention. He watched as a trio walked through the house, and the thermal image suddenly disappeared. Then, just as suddenly, it reappeared to silhouette three people skulking through the woods.

He was convinced that they were in pursuit of the sword. Exchanging the thermal imaging camera for night vision goggles, he inserted his gun into his holster and silently exited his car. He slipped into the woods and quickly picked up their trail. He would give them lee-way and let them lead him to his treasure. Then he would wield the sword, strike them dead, and begin his quest as Chairman of the Children of the Nephilim.

CHAPTER 18

⁂

AT THE CROSSES

After trudging through the woods for almost half an hour, the three-midnight investigators pushed through the last group of trees. Before them was an aging brick house with crosses along the front door lintel.

Dottie wondered, "Do you think those crosses are original construction, or do you think the Cross family had them added once they took residence? It just seems too sentimental for bitter Mr. Cross. The way everything else has fallen into place tonight, it wouldn't surprise me if one of Chief Saunhac's ancient spirits had a part in leading the original owners to include the crosses in their design. I guess it doesn't matter when or how the crosses came to be; we know we are at the Cross family home."

Bill removed a key from his pocket, unlocked the door, and ushered Dottie in, "Ladies, first." He hesitated as he debated the wisdom of turning on the lights in the event someone followed them, but flashlights wouldn't be enough to search the house thoroughly. He decided they would have to risk it. He flipped a wall switch and filled the room with blinding light.

Everything was in place as it was the day Mrs. Cross passed. Dottie stood in the center of the room and spun slowly, trying to take in everything at once. When the fireplace came into her view, she stopped suddenly, overcome with emotion. Displayed on the mantel, almost shrine-like, was an urn she remembered.

Tearfully, Dottie explained, "That's Simon's urn. His wish was that when he died, he wanted to return to Canada, to his family home. A casket was out of the question if he wanted his identity to remain a secret and keep his family safe. So, he opted for a cremation to conceal his remains for easy transport across the ocean. We had a funeral in England and buried an urn filled with sand. MI6 then transported his cremains to his family in a clandestine manner. I don't know what they told his parents. I do know, though, we honored his wishes and got him home.

"I can't leave him here like this, alone on a dust-littered mantel."

Han came over and put his arm around her shoulder, "How about we finish our mission, and then we'll discuss what arrangements to make. We'll make happen whatever you decide."

Taking the handkerchief Han offered her, Dottie wiped tears from her face and nodded in agreement.

They searched the first floor and the cellar and found nothing that suggested a secret hiding place or any clues to the sword's whereabouts.

They continued upstairs, each taking a bedroom. It made the most sense for Dottie to search Simon's room. Again, she had to shake back the emotion that threatened to overwhelm her and observe the scene as an objective MI6 operative, not a grieving widow. She examined each picture in the room, finding nothing hidden in the backs or on the walls behind them. She considered each piece of furniture. There were no hiding places on the headboard and footboard. She found nothing hidden between the mattress and box springs or under them. She scrutinized the seams of the mattress, finding them intact, dispelling any hope of discovering a clue there. Finally, she turned to the desk. It was exactly like the one she and Simon had in their home. Simon had designed it and built it to include a secret compartment. Maybe this one contained one, too.

Dottie hollered, "Guys! I think I've found something!" Bill and Han rushed into the room.

"Simon had a desk exactly like this in England. He designed it with a secret compartment. Let me check something." Dottie crawled into the kneehole and traced her fingers along all the panels until she found the concealed latch. She compressed it, and a hidden drawer slid open. Inside the drawer were two pictures. One was of Simon standing proudly in his military uniform. Dottie removed it and tenderly ran her fingers over his face.

"Look at this other picture. Simon is posing with his father in front of a cave entrance. I can see why Simon would save this memory because his father is actually smiling, but what if it's more? What if it's the clue we're hunting for?" Dottie handed the picture over for Bill and Han to examine.

Excitedly, Bill said, "I know where this is. It's a secluded cave in the backwoods here on the Cross property. Mrs. Cross allowed the chief to use it for Mi'kmaq ceremonies. That would be an appropriate place to conceal the sword, especially if the chief safeguarded other treasures there. Let's go spelunking."

After extinguishing all the upstairs lights, they clattered down the stairs to the first floor. Once in the vestibule, Bill double-checked that he had bolted the front door, and then, they paraded to the back of the house, switching off the remaining lights.

While they determinedly searched, von Krueger casually leaned against a tree and watched as lights blinked on all over the house. He chuckled as he considered how hard they were working, not realizing it was for naught. When they came out with the sword, he would claim Joyeuse as his and kill them.

Von Krueger came to full attention when the lights suddenly started going out. He watched intently as the upstairs went dark, and then the bottom floor lights went out one by one, marking a path to the back of the house. It appeared they were exiting out the back when they'd entered through the front. Something was up. Von Krueger emerged from his hiding place and cautiously approached the rear of the house. With his night vision goggles, he watched the trio jaunt across the property toward the backwoods. Like a nocturnal cat, he silently stalked his prey.

CHAPTER 19

THE CAVE

Once Bill, Han, and Dottie exited the house, their veteran combat skills took over. They communicated only with hand gestures and traveled in a single file line. Bill led their army of three, and Han guarded the rear. Dottie didn't need their protection but honored their need for chivalry and marched between them.

They plowed through bushes and side-stepped protruding roots, which was difficult in the late-night darkness. Their breathing became labored as they pushed up the steep incline. Finally, Bill signaled them to stop. They had arrived at their destination.

They cautiously entered the dark, damp cave as Bill swept the flashlight beam around the floor and walls and then along the top of the cave to make sure no immediate threats were present. The only danger perceived was the colony of bats suspended from the top.

So as not to disturb the bats, Bill kept the flashlight beam angled away from them. Spotlighting a circle of stones in the center of the floor, he said, "This is where the chief had some of his ceremonies. He appreciated the privacy, but, more importantly, he felt closer to his ancestors here."

Fading images on one of the walls caught Han's attention. He asked Bill to illuminate them. Sliding on his glasses, he closely examined the drawings and explained, "These are Mi'kmaq symbols, but they resemble Egyptian hieroglyphs. This symbol is similar to the hieroglyph that represents goodness and truth. These golden triangles painted above the heads symbolize the word 'God.' And notice this upside-down ankh. It's a key of life. Ash found the golden Egyptian ankh when he and Cordy were fighting the Children of the Nephilim." He looked over his shoulder and declared, "This has to be the right place."

They went farther into the cave and came to a fork. After a whispered discussion, they decided that Bill and Dottie would investigate the left fork while Han investigated the right. They would explore for thirty minutes, walk back to where the paths split, and share their findings.

Bill and Dottie entered their tunnel. As they went deeper into the cave, their path narrowed, threatening their safety. Dottie grabbed the back of Bill's belt, and they stepped one foot over the other because that was all the space they had. The angle of the path became more treacherous as it changed to a steep decline. Dottie released Bill's belt, and instinctively, they flattened against the wall, and side by side, they inched to the bottom.

Bill swung the flashlight beam over the floor, getting a bearing on their terrain. The light reflected off a shiny blackness in the distance, suggesting a pool of water. Bill started to advance to investigate, but Dottie tightly encircled her hand around his wrist and stopped him. "Turn off the flashlight, Bill. I believe I saw a subtle glimmering coming up from the ground."

Bill shut off the flashlight. Instead of the expected utter darkness, a fluorescent rainbow of lights emanated from the area of the pool of water.

As they walked closer, the lights increased in intensity and brightness, exposing more Mi'kmaq ancient markings. Bill said in a hush, "I don't know what's happening, but I think we must be getting close to the sword."

Easing to the pond's edge, they peered into the water to see the source of the light show. Just below the surface, there was a formation of rocks that resembled the shape of a mounded grave. Dottie leaned in and gently moved them apart to expose a beaming, water-tight chest. She and Bill carefully lifted it out and set it on the ground. Bill pried it open using the short-handled pry bar he carried in his backpack.

Inside was another chest emitting a bright blue light. They repeated their process of removing and opening it. A soft, gauzy fabric shrouded the treasure within. Dottie gingerly peeled it back with bated breath to unveil Charlemagne's battle sword, Joyeuse. Incredibly, they had found it! They had found Joy!

Bill reverently viewed the sword. "It's a wonder that Simon actually found this. He found another Pure of Heart treasure and buried it here to keep it out of the hands of the Children of the Nephilim.

"Dottie, there's a yellowed envelope tucked along the side of the sword." Bill withdrew the aging parchment and carefully handed it to her. He positioned the flashlight beam so they could read the writing on the front. Recognizing her name in Simon's stylized handwriting, she dropped down on a rock in disbelief. She wondered what message he was sending her from the grave. Staring and stalling wouldn't answer her question. She dug her dagger out of her fanny pack, unsheathed it, and delicately slid it under the flap. As gingerly as she unveiled the sword, she removed Simon's letter and lovingly unfolded it. She took a private moment to read the letter, process its contents, and then read it aloud to Bill.

My Darling Dottie,

This must be as surreal for you to read as it is surreal for me to write it as a dead man. Please understand that my decision to keep this secret is based on your and my parents' safety.

You are looking at another key of life, Charlemagne's battle sword, Joyeuse. Like all Pure of Heart treasures, it has magical powers when wielded by a Pure of Heart but is a curse of destruction and death to anyone who would use it for evil. The Nephilim never accept the truth that they will never wield these treasures. In their arrogance and narcissism, they believe that in their greatness, they can override the curse and compel it to advance their sinister agenda. Although we know they can never use these relics for their evil gain, we continue to search for them and stow them away so that the Nephilim cannot destroy them or tarnish their reputation when they don't get the evil upper hand they crave.

I fear the Chairman might melt down the sword if he doesn't gain the power he believes he deserves. That is why I hid Joyeuse.

I am hoping Bill and Han assisted you in locating this great relic. There are no two more remarkable men to whom I entrust my greatest treasure, you, Dottie. Please thank them for me.

Now, I leave Joyeuse's safety in your hands. If you think this remains a secure spot, return the sword to its watery catacomb. If not, Bill will assist you in locating another hideaway.

You are my greatest joy!

Take care, Darling, until we meet again.

I love you.

Simon

A booming voice bellowed, breaking the moment's tenderness, "Well, well, well. How touching! The elusive Dottie Cross, I presume."

Slowly turning as one, Bill and Dottie faced a victorious von Krueger pressing a gun against the back of Han's head.

CHAPTER 20

SHOWDOWN

"You there, drop your gun and kick it over here," ordered von Krueger, "or I will make his lovely wife a widow."

Bill reluctantly removed his pistol from its holster and slid it across the cave floor.

"Boys, this is the windbag who sat beside me on the plane, the one Aziza saw in her vision.

"We meet again, Mister...? I don't remember you telling me your name while boring me to tears with your art knowledge."

"Well, Dottie, or should I say Atropa Nightshade? We finally meet. I am Josef von Krueger. You and your former husband have been a bane to my existence. I have been searching for you and my treasure most of my life, but you have thwarted me at every turn.

"Imagine my surprise when Atropa Nightshade sashayed across the stage during a mediocre dinner theater performance, looking exactly like the Dottie Cross of days long ago. Madame, I must say, you have an excellent plastic surgeon, for you don't look any older today than you did in the 1940s."

Dottie planted her feet and indignantly retorted, "Plastic surgery?! I'll have you know that every inch of my skin is just as the Almighty blessed me. Quality skin care and clean, healthy living have served me well, more than I can say for you."

"Hold on a minute," Han interrupted. "There was an up-and-coming art student named von Krueger when I taught at the University of Kiel."

"You remember correctly, and I remember you as well. But I remember you more as a sleuth than a professor."

With disdain, Dottie snarled, "Are you one of the Chairman's minions, or did you serve Hitler?"

"I began my career working for Simon's classmate, the Chairman. Over the years, using legal and illegal means, I have advanced to head art historian and procurer of great artworks for the Chairman and his family. They continue to desire the sword to increase their power and influence. All this time, they thought I was working to locate it for them when I was searching for myself. They are all imbeciles. I am so much more deserving of being Chairman. Now, with the sword, I will do just that. With the Chairman's defeat and the destruction of many of the key Nephilim centers, the Chairman's family is dealing with in-fighting between the Children of the Nephilim and Dark Watchers as both factions pivot for control. While they are in turmoil, I will take the sword and claim my rightful place as Chairman of the Children of the Nephilim. I will rebuild bigger, better, stronger, and more powerful. Now, hand over the sword!"

"Hold onto your knickers, old man!" Dottie demanded. "How did you verify my identity?"

"Moles are such disgusting little animals, but they make excellent sources of information. Your Captain Baines and others were especially helpful. They confirmed your identity and whereabouts, and your new hire in housekeeping obtained your travel arrangements for me."

"She must be very resourceful to bypass the locks and security for our suite, and I never detected it. I may have to recruit her," Dottie retorted sarcastically.

"Enough of this incessant yammering! Han, move beside your compadre. Dottie, wiggle your over-sexed body to my sword and present it to me."

Cheekily, Dottie inquired, "Present you my over-sexed body? Or present you the sword?" As if flicking away irritating dust, she continued, "No matter. You aren't man enough to handle either one of us."

Von Krueger raged, "You are nothing more than a despicable harlot! I'd never tarnish my reputation with anyone like you. As for the sword, I will wield it in victory and finally fulfill my destiny."

"Oh sir, you suffer from delusions of grandeur," Dottie taunted. "You are making threats and demands when you are nothing more than a powerless prisoner in a dark cave. You have no understanding of this magnificent treasure. You are just a madman trying to reclaim the past glory of a long-ago famous king. You certainly will meet your end if you continue in this vein."

Von Krueger continued to rant, "You insubordinate, worthless, empty-headed trollop! You dare to provoke me with distasteful insults while I stand aiming a pistol at your friends? You call me mad when I have outwitted you at every turn? In your oblivion, you led me directly to my quarry. You and your band of warriors did all the work, but I will leave as the victor carrying the spoils."

To misdirect and create skepticism about the sword, Bill suggested, "Von Krueger, what makes you think this is the authentic Joyeuse? You know as an art historian that others have declared multiple swords to be Charlemagne's."

"Simon Cross was no idiot. He would not have used these extreme measures to conceal this sword if it hadn't been Charlemagne's battle sword. Furthermore, he wouldn't have sacrificed his life for a forgery or a replica.

"This conversation has become tedious. Dottie, bring the sword to me before I make those sweet twins fatherless."

Dottie slowly approached the chest containing the sword. As she drew closer, the light emitting from it started a gradual kaleidoscopic swirl of colors. She cautioned, "The legendary sword is mighty in the hands of a Pure of Heart, but it is poisonous to the wielder who is corrupt. I'm warning you, von Krueger. The sword could turn and annihilate you."

"Not according to the love story that I choose to believe. Charlemagne carelessly lost possession of the sword. Its location was unknown for years until a young female knight discovered it. She lifted the sword and stroked it affectionately as she admired its beauty. The sword fell in love with her because she appreciated its quality and craftsmanship, not what the sword could do for her. In some magical way, it communicated to her that if she chose to wield the sword in battle, she would be victorious as long as her heart stayed true to it and her battle intentions were honorable. Sword in hand, she was fearless in battle, killing all who came against her.

"Charlemagne heard of her success and realized she had found his sword and was using it. He hunted her down and took it from her, but when he lost battle after battle, he realized the sword had forsaken him. Blaming his losses on the girl, he killed her, thinking the sword would return its allegiance and serve him. To his dismay, the broken-hearted sword pined for the young knight and her pure heart and never honored Charlemagne again.

"In an extraordinary dream, I saw that I am the female knight reincarnated. Therefore, Joyeuse is rightfully mine. I will not be fool-hearty like Charlemagne and treat it frivolously. I will treasure it, for I love Joyeuse, and it loves me. Together, we will rule the world."

"There's just one itty-bitty problem with your tale of delusion, von Krueger," Dottie pointed out. "That courageous young woman was a Pure of Heart, making it possible for her to wield the sword. If you try, you face certain death."

Furious, von Krueger swept the pistol barrel from Han and aimed at Dottie. She hurled the dagger she had concealed and impaled von Krueger's arm. Dropping his gun, he shrieked in excruciating pain, waking the bats. Irritated, they gathered as a vast black cloud and swarmed him, knocking him to the ground, then flew out of the cave away from the screaming heap.

He clumsily grabbed his gun, staggered back to his feet, and re-sighted his aim at Dottie. She leaned in, firmly gripped the pommel, and raised the exquisite sword from its resting place. She pointed the glowing tip toward von Krueger, and as if Dottie and the sword had become one, she declared, "Justice arise, and behold all the power of the heavens."

Mesmerized, von Krueger marveled at the gleaming sword. As he outstretched his hands to claim the treasure he yearned for, Joyeuse ignited and blasted a lightning bolt of massive energy. His marvel turned to astonishment as the electric charge penetrated his body. He dropped to the ground with his shocked, disbelieving, dead eyes fixed on the sword. Standing over his scorched body, Dottie growled, "I warned you."

CHAPTER 21

ALL IS WELL

Dottie reverently returned Joyeuse to its resting place. "Thank you, dear friend. You remain a valiant defender of humankind and once again answered the call of duty." She lovingly drew the gauzy cloth back over the sword as its light gradually dimmed. Bill and Han respectfully replaced its lid, settled it into its waterproof case, and restored it to its original underwater hiding place.

Their solemn task completed, they turned and dispassionately eyed the corpse. Han wondered, "What are we going to do with the body? Should we notify the local authorities?"

Dottie answered, "And tell them what, Han, that I disarmed von Krueger by striking him with a dagger and then killed him with a magic sword that shoots lightning bolts? They will never believe such a fantastical tale, and we don't want to draw attention to this place or its concealed treasure."

Bill nodded. "Dottie is correct, but more importantly, the

Mi'kmaq consider this a sacred cave. Leaving his remains to de-compose in this holy place would be sacrilege to all that Chief Saunhac and the tribe represent.

"None of us have cell phone reception here. I'll hike up to the cave entrance and contact Bob for a Light Watchers clean-up crew. I'll wait for their arrival and lead them back here."

Fifteen minutes later, alerted by caller I.D., a sleepy but alarmed Bob answered, "It's three o'clock in the fricking morning, Bill! This can't be good. What's happened? Is Cordy all right?"

"Yes, Cordy is fine. We have a situation here that requires your Light Watchers CEO's assistance. Han, Dottie, and I had an alter-cation with a Nephilim operative tonight named von Krueger. He's dead! We need a clean-up crew to remove his body and make his presence in our area disappear immediately. Also, he probably left a car near Chief Saunhac's house. We need it located and disposed of too."

"Since that is Chief Saunhac's and Cordy's neck of the woods, I always have an emergency team at the ready. I'll have a crew there in less than thirty minutes. Send your coordinates. How did von Krueger get to Nova Scotia?"

"By plane. He followed Dottie, managed to sit beside her, and attempted to pump her for information. I assume the car is an air-port rental."

"Great. I'll send a second team to locate the car. Have one of the clean-up crew send me a photo of the dead S.O.B. I'll arrange for a look-alike to return his rental and fly back to his home. The impersonator will disappear in a security blind spot in the airport. When von Krueger doesn't come home after disembarking, it will be up to the hometown authorities to discover what happened to him."

"Thanks, Bob. That sounds perfect. I have another request. Would you do a Pure of Heart investigation on Dottie to officially include her in the annals of the Pure of Heart? It's a long story, so here is the short of it. Von Krueger was pursuing Charlemagne's battle sword, Joyeuse, thinking he could use it to take control of the Children of the Nephilim and become the Chairman. Dottie's deceased husband found it long ago and concealed it in one of Chief Saunhac's caves. By coincidence, if you believe in that, we searched for the sword tonight and discovered it buried underwater. Von Krueger followed us, and in his attempt to take it from us at gunpoint, Dottie wielded the sword and killed him."

Bob incredulously responded, "The Pure of Heart considers Charlemagne's battle sword one of their treasures, so only a Pure of Heart can wield it. Since Dottie did just that, it verifies she is a Pure of Heart. That explains how she keeps intersecting with us when we're in conflict with Dark Watchers or the Nephilim. I'll get on that investigation right away."

"This is just a heads-up as you delve into your research concerning Dottie. She is very cagey when discussing her age, as she never answers the question," warned Bill.

"Isn't that interesting? Our Dottie is quite a mysterious woman, isn't she? I'll see what threads I can pull and where they lead me. One way or another, I'll get the information necessary to verify her Pure of Heart status for the official Light Watchers records."

"It'll be interesting to hear what you discover about our Dottie. She is one special woman, regardless of what you find or don't find. Thanks again, Bob, for taking care of all this. I'll wait for the crew and lead them to the clean-up site. Talk to you soon."

Once the cleanup crew finished their task, Bill looked around to assure the cave was as pristine as they found it. There was no remnant of von Krueger anywhere. The chest remained dark under its casket of stones. Bill called Han and Dottie over to the sword site and chanted a Mi'kmaq cleansing prayer to remove the stain of von Krueger's evilness and another to protect the contents buried in the water. Once they completed the rites, the weary band of warriors returned home.

As they entered the kitchen, three anxious loved ones swooped upon them, asking concerned and curious questions. The warriors were too exhausted to discuss the evening's events and assured them all was well and that they would discuss it later in the morning. Han thanked Cordy and Ash for staying up with Aziza and said, "I'm not as young as I used to be. These late-night maneuvers are for younger men. Come along, Aziza. Let's go to bed. I need a few hours of sleep before the twins get up." Ever the gracious hostess, Aziza reminded Bill and Dottie of the prepared lower-level guest rooms. Embracing Han's hand, they walked upstairs, followed by Ash and Cordy.

Bill concurred, "Han has it right. It has been an extremely eventful night. I am too tired to walk another step. I'll just sleep right here in this recliner." He dropped into the chair, stretched out, and was instantly asleep.

Dottie was restless and planned on leaving before the troops got up, so she showered and prepared for her departure. Not wanting to spoil the bed sheets for a few hours of sleep, she tiptoed to the living room and stretched out on the sofa. In mere moments, she was asleep, too.

CHAPTER 22

TIME TO GO

As Dottie dreamed of sweet days gone by, someone rudely jostled her shoulder. Keeping her eyes shut tight, she relished shooting the bloody asshole who dared disturb her. Reluctantly, she squinted through bleary eyes to see the handsome, red-haired angel with sword blazing standing imperiously over her. In a gravelly voice, she barked, "Turn that thing off before you wake Sleeping Beauty over there! What in the hell do you want? I need my beauty sleep!"

"I assume you remember me," stated Uriel. The light gleaming from the sword illuminated the same ageless face of the man who helped her find Han in the freezing waters.

Now fully awake, Dottie shielded her eyes and said, "Hello, Uriel. Even though it was many years ago, I remember your pinpoint laser vision that led us to rescue Han. On top of that, how could I forget those chiseled cheeks, that silky red hair, and your flaming sword? Come on, big guy, do a girl a favor and turn down the glow on that thing. My sunglasses are in my purse, so if you don't intervene soon, I'll be blind, and then I won't be able to goggle your manly physique."

Chuckling, Uriel tapped his sword, and the offending light immediately dimmed to a soft glow. "Madam, you are as sassy as ever. I'm happy to see some things never change. I apologize for interrupting your slumber, but I need you to accompany me. I have something to show you that I believe will interest you."

Dottie stiffly arose and begrudgingly followed the irritating angel into Chief Saunhac's library, where she, Bill, and Han just the night before researched Charlemagne's sword. Had it only been a few hours ago? It felt like it had been eons. As she entered, she noticed an open steel case on the table that hadn't been there previously. She wandered over and took a curious peek. To her astonishment, it encased what appeared to be ancient stone tablets.

"These look like the tablets Chief Sanhauc told me about during one of our adventures." Dottie turned and pleadingly looked at Uriel, "No one here knows that I knew Chief Saunhac when he was younger. They have no idea that he and I completed Pure of Heart missions together.

"They know nothing about me, Uriel, but I suspect you do, considering your heavenly residence and who your boss is. Please keep my secret. It is not my time to answer their understandable questions."

"I do know, Dottie, and I understand there is a time and a place, and this isn't either one. I also understand the double-edged sword of honor and burden that you carry. Your adventures remain our secret.

"Now, for the real reason I'm here. I need you to take Remington's find and Charlemagne's sword to Bob so he can secure them in the secret facility that houses the rest of the Keys of Life and

Pure of Heart treasures. I'd take them myself and tip a bottle with him, but I have an assignment elsewhere. You, my fine lady, will shuttle these precious relics to Light Watchers headquarters. With your exquisite beauty, brains, and bite, we know you will safely transport and deliver them to his protective custody."

"Easy for you to say, Uriel. You're not the one who has to go back to the cave and get the sword. Once I get it out of its tomb, it's too heavy to carry alone."

"Don't get your pretty pantaloons in a roar, Dottie. I've already gone spelunking. The sword is right here, battened down, and ready to go. You don't have to do anything except get the treasures to Bob. Let's close up the tablets and prepare them for their journey."

Packing completed, Uriel handed Dottie Bob's business card. "This is the address for the headquarters. He's expecting you later today. I've already contacted your favorite taxi driver. He'll be here in the next hour. I've directed him to take you to this rental company where a car awaits reserved in your name." Uriel handed her another card. "The driver has already received payment for the fare with an exceptional tip included for his expedient services. All you have to do, Dottie, is get in with your charges and enjoy the ride."

"OK, I'll be your courier. I've already packed, so I am ready to go when the driver arrives. I just need to jot a note to my tribe since I'm leaving without saying goodbye. I don't want to appear ungrateful for their wonderful hospitality."

Dottie wrote:

Dear Family,

How precious it is to be able to call you all family. I must be off. Duty calls once again, preventing me from saying a proper goodbye.

Thank you all for making me one of yours. It has been my life-long desire to be part of an extended family. This is a true blessing.

Thank you, Aziza, for welcoming me into your home and sharing your generous heart with me.

Thank you, Bill and Han, for a night to remember. I know Simon is proud of us.

Hugs and snuggles to the little ones.

And, Ash and Cordy, don't let the sheets get cold.

Until we meet again,

Love to you all,

Aunt Dottie

There was a horn toot as she gently propped the note beside the still-sleeping Bill. Dottie grabbed her bag and marched outside while Uriel followed, effortlessly pushing a treasure-laden dolly. As the enthusiastic driver assisted Dottie and her cargo into the back seat, Uriel poked his head in with a final remark, "As always, Dottie, it has been a pleasure. I'm sure we'll see each other again. Safe journey." He shut the door, thumped the roof, and saluted the indomitable Dottie as she jetted down the road.

Once again, as the taxi sped along its course, Dottie quietly reflected on the past twenty-four hours. She acquired an extended family, visited her deceased husband's family home, discovered a long-ago buried Pure of Heart treasure, eliminated a homicidal maniac, and now was en route to deliver the relics to a secure facility. Leaning back in the seat, she contentedly smiled and thought, *all in a day's work.*

Chapter 23

EPILOGUE

As Dottie waited for her rental car to arrive, she called Major Dickey at MI6 headquarters. She hated to be the bearer of bad news, but it was necessary.

"Dottie, ole girl, how are you? I didn't expect to hear from you this soon. Why aren't you enjoying your family time?"

"We have a situation at headquarters, Major. I won't go into all the details right now, but it has come to my attention that there is at least one mole in our midst. Captain Baines divulged my identity and location in Nova Scotia to a stalker. I neutralized my unwanted shadow, but headquarters remains at risk. I need to return home for a quick turnaround with my hubby. Then, I will be on a plane to come and assist in ferreting out Baines and any other traitors."

Major Dickey sighed with resignation, "So it's true. We've suspected a mole in the agency for some time, but Baines was never a consideration. He covered his tracks well. Rest assured, Dottie, he has punched his timecard for the last time. He won't compromise anyone else. I welcome your assistance in uncovering any others. I'll create an identity so you can work your magic without anyone knowing why you're here. As always, darling, top-notch work."

Dottie drove to Light Watchers headquarters without a hitch. As she pulled into the portico, she approved of Bob's cleverness. The business front was a wealth-management corporation. Very few knew of the actual business conducted on the top floors.

A young doorman eagerly scurried toward her. Enjoying the naivety and enthusiasm of youth, Dottie decided the cutie needed a little tease. She adjusted the plunge of her neckline to accentuate her ample cleavage. She rolled down the window and feigned a southern drawl, "Why, aren't you a handsome one? I wonder if you could give me some assistance. Poor little ole me can't handle these heavy parcels." With that, Dottie opened her door and slowly extended one stiletto-shoed foot and then the other. She stood to her full height, straightened her back, seductively smoothed her dress over her curves, and was delighted as the young man ogled and blushed.

Momentarily speechless, he signaled with one finger to wait and ran inside. He quickly returned, pushing a dolly. He opened the back door and deftly stacked the two chests. Finally, finding his voice, he politely inquired, "Where would you like me to take these?"

"To the main elevator, please. Thank you for your studly assistance, young man," Dottie purred. With a flirtatious smile, she caressed his arm and handed him a generous tip.

Dottie, with dolly in tow, rode to the ninety-sixth floor. People dressed in business attire usually exited the elevator. When a blond bombshell pushing a handyman's dolly strolled out, all the receptionist could do was gawk at the unexpected visitor. Realizing she was not performing professionally, she stammered, "May I help you?"

Amused at the receptionist's discomfort, Dottie replied, "Yes, I have an appointment with Bob. My name is Dottie, but he might know me better as Dirty Dottie. He should be expecting me."

The befuddled receptionist buzzed Bob's office, "Sir, there's a Miss Dirty Dottie here. She says you are expecting her." Instead of a response from her employer, there was dead silence, and his office door flung open.

"Hello there, beautiful! Let me assist you with your buggy." Bob powerfully strode into the reception area and took control of the dolly. He wheeled it to his office as Dottie followed and admired his sexy backside.

"Have a seat, pretty lady. May I offer you a libation? Ice water? Something stronger?"

"No thanks, hot stuff. I'm anxious to get back on the road. My stud muffin is waiting for me to come home and light his oven. This little courier service wasn't exactly on my itinerary today. I still have an hour's drive to the airport."

"All right, then. Uriel contacted me regarding your precious cargo. I've put things in motion for their security." Locking eyes with her, he continued, "I understand you had a bit of an adventure acquiring the sword."

Nonplussed, Dottie returned his stare. "You can say that, but it's over and done with. It's in your hands now." Not wanting the conversation to go to topics she didn't want to discuss, she attempted to bring the meeting to a close, "If there isn't anything else, I need to go."

"Just one more thing. Uriel asked me to share these with you as a token of our appreciation for finding the sword and escorting the treasures here." Bob pulled open a drawer, retrieved two stones, and handed them to her.

"These are the Stones of Truth. You will find them helpful as you search for your mole or moles at MI6." Dottie looked at him, astonished that he knew about their security breach. "Our friend Uriel has vast knowledge. Anyway, if you place the stones in the vicinity of the person you are interviewing, they will move toward each other if they are telling the truth and away from each other if they are lying. They help me weed out Dark Watchers and Nephilim attempting to infiltrate our organization. Once you identify your traitors, please return the stones to me."

"Deal," and she extended her hand. "Thank you. I'm returning to headquarters at the end of the week to aid the investigation. Hopefully, I won't require their assistance for very long. Now, if there isn't anything else, I really need to go. I have a plane to catch."

"Of course, Dottie, Pure of Heart." Bob embraced her and tenderly placed a kiss on each cheek. "Safe travels, valiant one. We owe you so much personally and in our war against the Children of the Nephilim. You answer your calling well. Remember that your family loves you as you continue the fight for right. Return to us soon."

Dottie escaped before she broke into tears. She hurried to the elevator and was grateful for the ninety-six-floor descent to compose herself. When she reached the ground floor, the elevator doors opened, and a serene, dry-eyed Dottie exited and strutted confidently across the lobby to her car.

She opened her phone to find a voicemail message from her husband, "I miss you and can't wait to hear all about your latest adventure."

She returned his call and left her own message, "I miss you too. Lay out our favorite black teddy and get the fires burning! I'll be home soon, and I am raring to go. Love you!"

With a joyful heart, Dottie slid on her sunglasses, shook out her hair, and drove out of the portico, thankful for the past and looking forward to the evening and the adventures to come.

About the Authors

Carolyn Schield and Tom Vorbeck are number one bestselling authors—a unique brother and sister team who came together after drifting apart to combine their talents and co-write a thrilling, adventurous, and mysterious trilogy—*Keys of Life*. It has been a #1 Top 100 Amazon bestseller for historical fiction, historical thriller, and historical fantasy over and over again.

Carolyn writes articles for alternative media and international magazines. She lives in Texas with her husband and children.

Tom is an award-winning artist. His work can be seen at the Holocaust Museum in Washington, D.C. He lives in Missouri with his wife, Jennifer.

Carolyn and Tom hope to share their passion and excitement for life with their readers in their new series, *Adventures of Dirty Dottie*.

For more information, our readers can visit our website:
www.facebook.com/urielsjustice
www.amazon.com/Keys-Life-Justice-Carolyn-Schield-ebook/dp/B00JHV5TEK

www.ingramcontent.com/pod-product-compliance
Lightning Source LLC
Chambersburg PA
CBHW060126260626
47160CB00005B/2034